PORCELAIN

DOM HILTON

AFTER 18 YEARS
YOU ARE MEANT TO GIVE PORCELAIN ...

HERE YOU ARE!

xxy

Many thanks to Kate Feather and Natalie Terry.

"Once there lived a demon who had a peculiar diet: he fed on the anger of others. And as his feeding ground was the human world, there was no lack of food for him."

Based on the *Samyutta Nikaya*, Sakka Samyutta, No.22, translated by Nyanaponika Thera.

PART 1

1

The utility pole bristled with rusty staples and thumbtacks. He didn't want to have to get a shot, so he carefully spread the flyer across the gap between an ad for a handyman and a faded, missing dog. He had taken the picture on the poster, it was maybe his favorite. Angela was sitting by the window in her mom's studio, sunlight streaking her curly red hair and impossibly clear, green eyes. She was smiling, showing the prominent white teeth he liked to tease her about. The blocky text underneath he knew by heart; when she had gone missing, what she was wearing, who to call. How she was thirteen, like him.

The wind kicked up and he scowled as he struggled with the staple gun, it was too cold for just a t-shirt. A few specks of rain started to blur the print, he should have covered it in plastic. He jammed the staple gun back into the grocery tote with the remaining bundle of flyers and started jogging along the cliff path, the wind whipping the beach grass around him.

As the path curved around the headland, the squat grey bungalow came into view. He hesitated and dropped into a slow walk. He was disappointed to see the sway-backed, rusted, white F150 that belonged to his dad but it was the police car that made him feel really anxious. He paused, considering his options but the cold wind and the expectation of his mom's Tuesday night meatloaf pushed him towards home.

He quietly entered the side door into the kitchen, silently closing it behind him. He could hear voices from the living room, his mom was talking in that soft, breathless voice that always appeared when his dad was home from the rig. The other voice was female, kind of familiar, but he couldn't make out exactly what they were saying. He looked around the kitchen, the oven was off and no sign of the meatloaf. The grocery money was still sitting on the table on top of a shopping list. He gave a resigned sigh and opened the living room door.

The talking stopped immediately leaving only the moan of the wind against the eaves. His mom gave him a nervous, tight smile from her perch on the edge of the sofa, on the easy chair opposite he recognized Officer Willet from the trouble at school. Between the women, his dad stood staring out of the picture window at the white-capped, steely sea below. He did that a lot, he didn't seem to enjoy being home on leave from the rig, even though he said he hated his job. The frost of age had crept through the temples of his black, wavy hair but he was still a powerful man, filling the window frame. His jaw muscles clenched beneath his beard as he rubbed the brass Zippo in his right hand. He did not turn or speak a word, just lifted the tumbler of rum from the windowsill to his mouth.

Officer Willet stood up and smiled.

"Hi Coby, how are you holding up?"

"Okay, I guess."

"I'm so sorry about Angela, I know you two are good friends. Your mom says you've been helping with the flyers, is that right?"

"Yeah. I should've put them in plastic."

"Every little bit helps. Listen, Coby, I'm here because I'm going to need to ask you a few more questions, is that okay?"

He looked from his mom's worried face to his dad's silent back.

"I guess".

"Good. Now, you told Officer Nunes that you last saw Angela on Tiskill Beach, on Sunday afternoon around 4pm, right?"

"I guess, yeah."

"Remind me what you guys did."

"We were just talking and looking for stuff on the beach, then Angela went home for her dinner and I walked back along the path to my house."

"Did you go anywhere else?"

He hesitates a beat.

"No, I don't think so."

"There's a beached boat wreck on the rocks at the far end of Tiskill Beach, you know the one I mean?"

"Yeah."

"We found a blue coat inside that has your name in it, do you know how it got there?"

"No. I mean, I lost it. I think."

Officer Willet's gaze didn't falter, she was letting him dig his own hole with her silence. His knees started to tremble, he saw his dad put his glass back on the windowsill and start to turn.

Something took over inside Coby and he spun backwards, bursting into the kitchen. He snatched up the grocery money as he ran for the back door, wrenching an old plaid work jacket from the coat stand in the hall as he flung himself into the cold outside. He could hear the rising adult voices behind him as he pumped his legs along the path, lowering his head into the roaring wind. He ran until it was pitch dark and he was truly lost.

2

He felt the blast of heat on his face as he bent down to slide the peg into the peephole on the side of the kiln. He adjusted the heat setting and stood to stretch. Like often happened when he checked the time on the clay-spattered wall clock, he was surprised that a whole afternoon had been absorbed by the dry-mouthed focus of his work. The studio was empty, he'd hoped it would be, and he stretched again in the dusty hot air that floated around him in silence.

The studio door swung open accompanied by the faint chittering of ear-buds. It was Dylan, or Elon, he couldn't remember the name. There was a lot of scarves and facial hair, and a laundry basket with a clay head.

"Hey, Man. Just firing it up, right?"

"Yeah, I guess."

"Hey, heads-up, Prof Lutkin is looking for you, doing the rounds."

"Okay, thanks, Elon."

"Dylan."

"Yeah, sorry."

He started quickly packing his things into a backpack and had just shouldered it to leave when the door swung open again. A gnomish man with wispy black hair and an improperly buttoned cardigan strode in with a sense of purpose.

"Ah, Jay, I was hoping to catch you."

"Yeah, I'm afraid I have to go right now. Sorry."

"Won't take a moment, let's step into my office."

Prof Lutkin was clearly in no mood to be trifled with and held the door open with a chin-tilt of defiance. Jay dropped his head in surrender and walked out into the corridor.

The office was cramped and overstuffed, what little floor space there was being encroached by shifting stacks of books and papers. Jay slid into a shabby mid-century chair and looked out at the surprisingly impressive view of the city. Professor Lutkin creaked back in his chair and petted his wispy beard as he scanned through his laptop screen.

"I'm missing three assignments from you, you are skipping classes and I've yet to get a reply to any message I've sent you. You had such a strong start to the semester, what is going on, Jay?"

"I'm just trying to get that one piece finished, then I will catch up"

"What piece?"

Jay felt a twinge of irritation at the man's brow, wrinkled in deep concern. Jay cleared his throat.

"Ceramics".

"Why are you still working on that module? That was due months ago. I've seen dozens of your pieces on the shelves, all very similar, you just need to submit one and I can give you an extension for the write-up."

"I just need to get it right but, yeah, I'll do that."

The professor's nose wrinkled in anger and a vein stood out on his temple.

"If you obsess over this any longer I won't be able to save you from failing. You have a full scholarship, so you understand what that means?"

Jay gazed out of the window and watched a police helicopter skim the skyline. He looked back to see the professor's features have softened.

"Look, I know you went through a great deal this year with the, um, tragedy but it was you that wanted to continue with the semester."

Jay resented that Professor Lutkin knew about that. He was forced to tell him because he needed to miss exams while he took care of things. Thank god the attorney helped him sell the house and contents without him ever having to set foot in the place, he couldn't bear the idea. Professor Lutkin was giving him a look that seemed to convey admiration before sitting forward to continue.

"I really do respect your dedication but hard-paste porcelain is a challenging medium and you don't need to perfect it, we are just trying to give you some experience of different materials. Let's do this; turn in whatever you have tomorrow with the write-up and we can get you back on track but I won't be able to help if you don't, okay?"

"Okay. Thank you."

It was the professor's turn to stare out of the window, he looked sad, or maybe lost in an old thought. Jay left the claustrophobic office, passed the studio with a twinge of guilt, then descended into the dark, cool stairwell.

3

The sun was so warm he had to unzip his jacket, the sea was glassy and blue, it was perfect. He surprised himself by spinning a couple of times as he crossed the beach. The familiar hulk of the beached boat shimmered in the warming air, orange with rust and trimmed with long ribbons of glossy kelp still wet from high tide. Muscle memory carried him quickly up the side, his sneaker squeaking on the damp rim of a busted porthole. Once on the canted deck, he slowed down to descend the weedy rungs that led into the dark belly of the wreck. This was his secret place, his cool, quiet cave.

He moved carefully as his eyes adjusted. Painful experience had taught him that the edges of the boat's ribs and plates had been eaten by the saltwater into cruel, rusty blades. He reached into his jacket and found a plastic sandwich bag that contained some sausage patties he'd snuck from breakfast. Towards the rear of the lower deck was a large steel tank built into the deck. It was partially filled with sand, rocks and weed but the water was replenished with every high tide, like a rock pool. Even though it was tilted, the water was chest-deep on the lowest side.

Coby crumbled a patty into the water and a pale shape started to move from darkest, deepest corner of the tank. With it came the familiar scratchy rumble that seemed to come from the very center of his head.

The first time Coby had heard Kabu he was so confused, he just heard this weird sound that sounded like "Kabu" over and over until it led him to the tank and he saw him. He was magnificent, a huge horseshoe crab that was totally white. Coby had figured he was an albino. As soon as Coby had called the crab by his name out loud, Kabu had begun to speak to him. Not really speaking, it was more like a string of feelings and images over the top of the scratchy rumble, but it was clear to Coby. Kabu told him about the sea and the places he had been, all the brave things he had done. He asked that Coby keep him safe and secret because there were bad people that could kill him. Over the past few weeks since Coby had found him, he and Kabu had become close friends. Kabu wanted to know all about him and thought his ideas were cool while Coby loved to hear the recounted exploits of the cunning old crab.

Kabu moved towards the crumbles of patty that lay on the sandy floor of the tank, moving into a bright beam of light that had cut through the gloom from a porthole. His domed body was shockingly white in the sun, making the water around him glow.

As he ate, Kabu talked about Angela, how he wanted to meet her. Coby was kind of shocked, Kabu was a secret he had to protect, he never thought it was something he would have to share. Then again, as Kabu explained, Angela was someone he trusted, someone he really, really liked. He started to feel excited about how cool it would be to share this huge secret.

Coby made a solemn promise that he would do his best to bring her.

Coby emptied the last of the food into the tank, saluted goodbye, then made his way back up the slippery ladder into the bright light of the afternoon. He paused to squint feeling like he'd just come out of a movie theater, then jumped down onto the hard sand, a knot of excitement growing in his chest.

A pathway carved between the steep dunes that led up to a small lot by the road. Despite the good weather the lot was empty, it often was down at the far end of the beach. Coby followed the road to a small strip of houses. Miss Klein's cottage was the one right at the end, pale blue and surrounded by wildflowers. In the mudroom he added his sneakers to the short row of various footwear, and tapped the door knocker lightly. It was opened almost immediately by a short woman in a work smock, large glasses and a streaked auburn bun. She broke into a smile that was identical to that of her daughter. Boop the French bulldog skidded over the threshold yipping and bunting his calves.

"Hello, hello", said Miss Klein and beckoned him in.

Tilting her head up the staircase behind her, she called, "Angela, Coby is here."

Looking back at Coby, she asked, "Hungry?"

"Sure, yeah".

The cottage was bright and clean, and always smelled of good food and flowers. Whenever he returned home, he noticed that his own house smelled of damp carpets and stale cigarettes. He wondered if he smelled of those things to Angela. He followed Miss Klein into the kitchen where she started putting some fresh-baked cheese turnovers onto a couple of plates with sliced apples.

"We should finish your comic book today, right?"

Coby nodded as he took a bite of the pastry. It was so good.

"You have such an amazing imagination, Coby. I was thinking we could screen-print a cover, make it look super pro."

Miss Klein used to be his teacher at the middle school. One day, after the troubles at school, she had asked him if he wanted to come over on Sundays for tutoring. She sent a note home for his mom saying she wouldn't have to pay anything. Coby liked Miss Klein but it felt weird seeing a teacher outside of school. He soon realized that it wasn't the kind of tutoring he thought it would be. They did cool projects with lots of talking and snacks, not more homework. She had these amazing books he could borrow, like the cool samurai history book he was reading, which had lots of gory fights. He enjoyed writing and art the most but the talks were good too. He hoped he'd always be able to go to the cottage.

He heard a familiar sequence of squeaks from the stair treads and Angela slid into the kitchen on her socks. She bashed into him and plucked up her turnover. She was wearing her surf green sweatshirt and she smelled good too, like laundry detergent and something powdery. He sneaked a sniff of his t-shirt but it smelled normal. She smiled at him and he nearly blurted it out but just smiled back, enjoying the secret he held.

Coby was working on the final showdown spread in his comic book. The hero was a boy his age who had found a strange doll washed up on the beach. The little man had a ragged, red suit and horns on his pale, bald head. At first he was just a doll, but then he came alive to help the boy beat the bullies with powerful voodoo magic. Coby had drawn him with small blank eyes and a very slightly curved mouth so it was hard to tell if he was happy or scary. Miss Klein said it was enigmatic like the Mona Lisa. Coby had called him Kabu after his friend.

Angela looked over from the ship-in-a-bottle she was working on. She had made a bunch of them and they were getting really good, he had a couple at home in his bedroom. Her mouth dropped open when she saw the panel.

"That looks awesome!"

Coby tried not to blush and played it cool.

"Thanks. He's turning all the bullies into zombies with really gross zits and making them dance super lame at the middle school dance."

Angela started giggling, so he threw in a few lame zombie dance moves to keep her going.

"But then he turns mean so the boy has to throw him back in the sea."

Angela's giggles faded away when he said this.

"That seems pretty sad."

Coby shrugged as Miss Klein breezed into the room with something covered in a dishtowel. Angela and Coby turned to watch her, curious about the bundle.

"I did it, guys! Finally got one fired perfectly."

She dramatically drew the cloth from a white ceramic pony that she set down in front of Angela's wide eyes. Coby felt a little flash of jealously that Miss Klein had taken Angela's attention from him but had to admit the sculpture was amazing. Sitting in a shaft of afternoon sunlight, the translucent glaze shimmered, one front leg slightly lifted to meet the curve of its dropped neck. It was beautiful.

"Mom, that is so lovely! Can I keep it?"

Miss Klein gave a delighted laugh and squeezed Angela's shoulder.

"It was meant for you, silly! Just be careful with it because it's very fragile."

"I will, thank you, mom."

Miss Klein turned to Coby, maybe sensing that he was feeling a little left out.

"Mister Coby, I will be right back with my screen and materials so I can show you how to print. We can figure out a design for your cover and maybe make a couple of t-shirts too."

"That sounds cool."

Coby smiled and watched her leave, then slid low over the table to whisper to Angela.

"Hey, later, do you want to come with me somewhere secret?"

Angela looked up from her pony with an expression he hadn't seen before, one that thrilled him someplace deep inside.

4

The further Jay got from campus, the more the guilt seemed to dissipate, joining a grey morass of general unease and overlapping, threadbare promises. He floated through the clumps of teens on screens, middle-aged couples who still talked to one another and podcasting dog walkers. He had the pleasant gnawing of a hunger sure to be sated as he left the main arteries of the city for the capillaries of the Northern back-streets.

Jammed between an auto repair shop and a tile supply store, the tiny grocery didn't even have a name. Some rough plywood shelves held stacks of produce, some recognizable to Jay, some not so much. The single window was layered with so many stickers for phone cards, cigarettes and scratch-off cards, it was no longer a functioning window.

He stepped into the fluorescent hum of the interior. The young girl perched on a high stool behind the gum displays on the counter flicked her eyes at him, realized she wasn't needed and went back to her phone. Jay slowed to allow his vision to adjust as he walked further back into the deep shadows of the store. He could hear a low mumble of male voices and the soft click of chess pieces as he passed stacks of copper pots and sacks of rice. The spicy aroma of the kahwah tea mingled with tobacco smoke as he walked through the store room. Like the girl out front, the huddle of men around the game table barely looked at him. He continued further back through a small loading dock stacked with boxes and knocked on an unmarked door in the corner with three, two, then three more taps. After a few minutes, the door opened a crack. Satisfied, the young man inside opened the door and nodded his head to the stairs behind him, Jay followed him inside.

Valy was a little older than Jay, an impeccably groomed, handsome Afghani who eschewed traditional dress for conspicuously branded streetwear and intricate barbering. Jay liked him a lot but was aware of a cooling between them in recent weeks.

"You gotta get a phone, bro, lemme know you comin'. I could be taking care of somethin' else."

"Sorry, man, can't do it. Why, something going on?"

Valy does a little head waggle and sucks his teeth.

"My uncles are not happy, they wanna go more refined, more delivery. Hipster chandu scene is dying off, bro."

Jay didn't like the sound of that at all. He'd hoped he could always come to the lounge, it was his place.

"So, I'm a dying hipster now?"

Valy didn't reply but pulled back a curtain on a large loft space above the store. There was no natural light, only strings of tiny lights around the lattice of beams and ropes that were used to hang heavy blankets and kilims. This created small dark cells, each with an army surplus cot and side table, but tastefully done with traditional pillows and patterned fabrics. All of them seemed to be empty but the telltale smell of incense tinged with a sour fishiness told Jay he was probably not alone. He walked into his usual corner spot and shucked off his backpack before stretching on the edge of the cot like he was about to take a nap. As he plumped the pillow and stretched out on his back, Valy came in with the layout tray and slid it onto the low table beside Jay. With a ceremonial practice at odds with his baseball cap and appliqué t-shirt, he lit the oil lamp and used the antique tools to work up a pill-shaped piece from the sticky, black block.

This is what had seduced Jay that evening a few years ago. He was not a sociable student but the art crowd had some relentless scenesters and he got sucked into an evening that had begun at a basement punk show, made an ironic detour to a strip club, then landed at a loud girl's slick apartment. After some drinks and barkering from the loud girl, Valy appeared with a cool smile and a beautifully ornate layout tray. With the deep knowledge and confident wit of a hip professor, he had taken them through the cultural and spiritual highlights of opium. He walked them through the antique lamp, his collection of porcelain and jade bowls, mysterious tools and, finally, the intricately carved pipe. Jay was intrigued by the ceremony but when he drew the thick smoke into his lungs and felt the World fall away, he knew this was a beginning of something new. After all the scenesters had taken a turn, some acting nonchalant and one guy getting sick, the evening began to wind down and the pipe was discarded on the inlaid tray. Jay introduced himself to Valy and learned about the lounge, without a second thought he had made plans to go, and go he did. He lost long afternoons, sometimes blissfully drifting into the next day. Back then, the place had an exclusive coffee shop feel, populated by traveler-type couples and bearded young men with notebooks or headphones. One girl described it as feeling like the hash cafes in Amsterdam. Over time those people fell away but Jay preferred the quieter atmosphere with the few remaining regulars. He liked his secret, quiet cave.

Valy sat back on his heels as he finished rolling the pill and picked up the needle.

"You comfy, man? I gotta split."

"Wait. I have something for you."

"Ah, ok."

Jay reached into his backpack and pulled out a white, segmented pipe with small white bowl attached to the side. He carefully handed it to Valy.

"I made it, it's porcelain."

Valy turned the pipe in the light, frowning at the biomorphic form. The rim of the bowl was surrounded by petal-shaped plates lined with spines, closing around a deep spiral groove on the underside that ended at the smoke hole. Jay could tell he wasn't into it.

"Yeah, that's sick, bro. Thanks. I think you should christen it though."

He used the needle to work the pill onto the bowl, then handed the pipe back to Jay, nodding with unconvincing approval.

"Looks sick, man. See you on the flip."

Jay took the pipe and repositioned the lamp before getting comfortable. Valy slipped out of the cave and pulled the blanket closed behind him. It snagged on the rope so it was still open a sliver. This bothered Jay but as he drew the thick smoke into his hungry lungs, it bothered him less and less.

5

The wind was roaring through the trees and the road was absolutely black in front of him. He was scared and tired, he thought about going home. He thought about meatloaf, he thought about his dad and the money he stole off the table. He pulled the baggy work jacket tighter around his shivering chest and leaned into the unrelenting gusts.

With a distracted sense of relief, he watched the road ahead brighten in front of him, seeing the crest of a hill and some wind-tossed leaves. Realizing that it was from car headlights coming from behind, that inner mechanism punched through his weariness and flung him into the hedgerow by the roadside. Sharp twigs cut into his face and a thorn drove painfully into his right knee as he buried himself into the dank leaf litter under the bushes. The car slowed down and his heart hammered in his throat. Peering up over his forearm he could see the livery of the police car. A spot light swept slowly over the bushes, he tucked in his feet and buried his face in his elbow. There was the hum and squeak of an electric window being lowered.

"Coby? Coby? This is Officer Willet, come on out, son. Everything is fine, we just want you home safe with your family."

Coby pushed his face deeper into the leaves, pulling in every part of his awkward body to be as small as possible. A lull in the wind allowed him to hear Officer Willet sigh. The car moved on and let out a few ragged breaths then forced himself to crawl back towards the roadway. The deep jab of pain in his knee pushed him onto his side with a gasp. He slid his hand down his jeans to find a sticky nub just under the kneecap. He found purchase with his thumb and forefinger then wrenched out the thorn, allowing himself a yelp.

He straightened to stand then froze when he saw the tail-lights of the police car a quarter mile up the road on the crest of the hill. He shrunk back towards the bushes and watched the spot light scan the verge. Snatched by the wind he could still just hear Officer Willet make the same plea, word for word. This made him feel a little better but also a little more guilty at the same time. A double-dip feeling as Miss Klein would say. He watched the SUV drop over the crest before he cautiously followed. When he reached the high-point of the road he saw a harbor town laid out in front of him that seemed familiar.

There was a small ferry terminal and a fishing harbor, a few houses and closed stores but not much else. The brightly-lit waiting room of the ferry terminal looked deserted and warm. There was also a vending machine in one corner. He figured he could warm up and get a candy bar until he figured out what to do next. Keeping close to the verge and scanning for police cars, he made his way down the steep hill to the windswept parking lot. His knee was beginning to throb and he felt very exposed. Before he could reach the terminal building, a coach pulled up to the curb and a noisy tide of chattering teenagers with identical backpacks spilled onto the curb with several tired-looking adults. The adults pointed to the terminal and shouted at the kids urgently in what might have been Italian. A deep horn drew Coby's attention to a small ferry turning into the dockside. He got swept up by the chattering kids as he pushed through the entranceway to the terminal lounge. Inside, an unshaven man in a back uniform and high-visibility vest walked towards the group as he talked to someone on his walkie-talkie. Coby stiffened and quickly scanned the parking lot. The man walked up to the two adults, who seemed to be teachers, and nodded to their questions, waving them through the departures gate. Noticing Coby hanging back, the man frowned and beckoned him over. Coby looked at his feet as he walked and saw that his jeans were bloodied around the rip in his knee. When he glanced up, the man was yawning and just waved him though the gate with the last of the Italian kids.

Coby didn't have a better plan, so he followed the last clump of kids up the gangway to the passenger deck as the empty coach drove onto the vehicle deck below. The harried male teachers guided the students into the rows of seats on the starboard side of the deck and Coby slipped into the final row on his own, just in case the walkie-talkie guy came back. A dark-eyed girl in the seat in front of him turned to look at him. She looked at him blankly, perhaps expecting to see a class-mate, then quickly took in his oversized jacket and bloody knee before pivoting back to her rapid conversation with the girl next to her.

With a deep shudder the ferry moved off from the dock and churned across the harbor. One of the teachers staggered down the aisle passing out white paper sacks to the rows of kids. When he reached Coby he looked momentarily confused, then presumably relieved that he did not recognize him as one of his students and walked away shushing what sounded like complaints from some of the kids. The dark-eyed girl leaned between the headrests to offer Coby her bag. He smiled and shook his head, but she pushed it closer to him with a very specific kind of hand shimmy that said it was not a big deal. He smiled and said thanks. She smiled back then ducked out of sight.

There was an apple, water, a granola bar, a bag of cheese crackers and a large, crusty roll wrapped in foil. He bit into the tuna sandwich and realized how hungry he was, the water he finished even faster. By now, the ferry had left the harbor and was hit by the full force of the wind-tossed sea. As the boat crested its first large wave a handful of kids whooped, one or two whimpered. Coby was used to being on boats and found the rise and fall comforting. As he drifted towards sleep, a memory surfaced of mom laughing as she tried to dance on the deck of a pitching cruiser, out on the bay some summer afternoon long ago. A shadow fell across her face and the laughing stopped, the same shadow pulled Coby into a haunted, fitful sleep.

6

It was a world beyond sleep, shifting with amorphous grey landscapes and shadowy forms. He could feel that the spell was wearing off and he reluctantly allowed himself to drift up to the surface. His eyes slowly focused on the small string of lights on the ceiling. His throat was very dry and his limbs felt like stone. He eased his head sideways to rest on his cheek and his gaze fell on the annoying gap in the curtain. Across the walkway was a cubicle that also had a gap, which lined up with his. He could just see the top half of a figure lying on the cot, facing away from Jay. The figure was wearing a jacket of very coarse, red fabric, almost like burlap. The thick, black stitching was exaggerated and clumsy, the one button Jay could see on a side pocket was comically large. He wondered if the person was a street performer or an actor. A small movement drew his attention to the back of the figures head, there was an undulating flutter of something within the thick curls of greasy, black hair. Jay squinted, trying to make sense of the movement. Just as he assumed the figure had buried its fingers into its hair to scratch its scalp on both sides, the figure stretched out a thin arm and cupped the elbow with the other hand. Both hands were covered by black woolen mittens, another huge button hung from the ragged cuff. The strange, finger-like paddling on the figure's scalp continued.

Valy chose this moment to sweep into the cubicle with an agitated energy, blocking Jay's view of the figure.

"Hey, bro, how's things?"

Valy was distracted, thumb-swiping his phone and biting his nails.

"I'm good. Everything okay?"

It was unusual for Valy to interrupt like this. After a long pause he looked up from his phone.

"Yeah, man, just these changes and shit. Actually, I need to clear the place out. There's a family meeting."

Something felt weird and Jay's concern must have showed on his face.

"It's chill, don't worry. You know, I can always hook you up with a little take-out."

"Valy, man, you know my rules, only here and only at weekends. You're a bad enough influence already."

Jay tried a dry chuckle but Valy was back on his phone and didn't reciprocate. Jay cleared his throat as if that had been his intention all along.

"So, yeah, Jay, I'm gonna have to ask you to bounce. That cool?"

"Sure, I got some stuff to do, it's cool."

Valy left without looking up from his phone. Jay was relieved that the red-jacket figure had gone from the cot and the lounge was silent. He hauled himself upright and stood, stretching out before sliding on his backpack. He looked down at the porcelain bowl he'd made, still attached to the pipe, and felt a mix of emotions. Embarrassment but maybe also some resentment.

He shouldered through the fire exit in the loading dock and squinted into the bright, flat glare of the afternoon. Behind the auto-shop, a sinewy, old guy was smoking while he pounded on the wheel he was squatting over. The broken sidewalk was greasy and the gutters were choked with trash. Jay crossed the street to get away from the depressing alley and into the green, quiet of the church yard opposite.

This shortcut usually lifted his spirits as he followed the red brick path under the yew trees, past a small Norman church surrounded by weathered headstones. Today, the silence was split open by the exuberant pealing of bells. Jay followed the path around to the front of the church where a crowd of people were cheering on the steps. Confetti swirled around the heads of a flushed young couple as they grinned and waved their way down the steps. Jay tried not to feel cynical as he took in the fussy dress and the excess of product in the man's fresh haircut. They were happy and, Jay assumed, in love.

That part of him seemed walled off and he found it hard to understand in others. Early on, he'd tried dating at college but once the conversation had ended the expectation of what was supposed to happen next panicked him. It was like watching a wonderful play but then being yanked from the audience and asked to emote convincingly on the stage while completely naked. He did not see why people felt the two pursuits had to be coupled.

He skirted around the suits and hats and the waiting white limo, feeling a dark mood settle into him. He joined the flow of people on the street heading into the city for the evening. He saw the excitement of the young people in their loud conversation and exaggerated movements, their overthought clothes and cartoonish make-up. He'd been in the city so long but he never once felt excited about being there. He skirted past the group of kids in front of him, not minding that his shoulder connected hard with the kid that mock-staggered in front of him to get attention from his friends. The kid started shouting expletive-filled questions but went quiet when Jay simply slowed his walk. Jay enjoyed the feeling more than he wanted to admit.

Maybe he was hungry. When he reached the pedestrian plaza by the campus he walked over to the little ramen stand he liked. Jay held up four fingers to indicate to the guy in the truck that he wanted the Tokyo-style bowl. The assistant slid disposable chopsticks, paper napkin and bottled water over the counter, and took Jay's money in return. Jay found an empty table and killed the water in three long pulls. He let his head stay tilted back to watch the roiling underbelly of a thunderstorm making its way across the horizon.

The truck assistant interrupted his gaze with the bowl of noodles, giving a polite, swift bow. Jay pulled the bowl closer and snapped apart the chopsticks. He poked around the glazed half-egg, sliced pork and and the little dumpling with the pink spiral in the center, before pinching up a clump of steaming noodles from the broth. He slurped them gently into his mouth, looking forward to the comforting umami flavor. Instead, the noodles sat in his mouth like salty dishwater. He tried a piece of the pork but had to spit out the greasy, gristle-filled piece. The chef looked over at him from the hatch in the truck. Jay didn't care, the place seemed to have taken a dive in quality, he planted his chopsticks in the center of the bowl and stood to leave. The chef sent the assistant scurrying out to intercept him, but Jay stepped around the hand-wringing youth and walked away.

The brutalist facade of the arts building was not a welcome sight but Jay forced himself to cross the lobby and take the stairs. He was relieved that the studio was quiet and went over to the cooled kiln. Lifting the top with a familiar crackle of nerves in his chest, he gently picked up the piece inside and stood to inspect it in the light. He held his breath, turning it through every angle, finally standing it carefully on the work bench in front of him. It was perfect, absolutely perfect. His shitty mood drained out of him and he felt his throat thicken with emotion.

Standing at only eight inches tall, this shimmering piece of porcelain had consumed him for months. An abstract quadruped with fine curving legs, a torso of interleaved plates and spines, and a blunt head with minimalist features. The form hit the exact notes Jay had hoped for. It was strong but vulnerable, it was proud without being judgmental, it felt both prehistoric and futuristic. It was the first time Jay had made something that didn't scream out its shortcomings, it was the first time he had made something of which he was truly proud.

He pushed the wheeled discard bin over to the work shelves. At the furthest end there was a section on the top shelf that was labeled with his name. Like a small scale Terracotta Army, dozens of white quadrupeds stretched to the back wall in rows, each slightly different but all tainted by imperfection. Some had awkward curves, others small cracks from firing or slightly collapsed legs from being inadequately supported. Jay gleefully snatched them up, two at a time, and slam-dunked them into the bin. The delicate figures exploded with a satisfying hiss and tinkle of shards. Jay was about halfway through the shelf when Professor Lutkin ran into the studio looking startled.

"Jay! What the hell are you doing?"

"Cleaning up."

"That is your work, right?"

Jay could see from the panicked look in the man's eyes that the professor had thought this was some sort of melt-down. Jay gave him a tight smile.

"Yes, of course. I have what I need."

Professor Lutkin relaxed a little but continued to stare at Jay with suspicion. He looked over to the quadruped on the bench behind Jay.

"Is that your submission piece?"

Jay nodded and followed the professor over to the bench. The professor scratched at his wispy jowls and tilted his head.

"I have to say, that is very good."

He walked around it and tilted his head the other way.

"Yes, very good."

He seemed transfixed then abruptly changed gear with a cough.

"And the write-up, that's done too?"

Jay stifled a groan and sighed instead.

"Nearly, yes."

The professor picked up the quadruped and gently turned it in his hands, squinting at the details on the plates. Satisfied, he carefully placed it back down on the bench.

"Remarkable. Well, send me the write-up tonight by midnight, okay? Then we shall get you back on track."

Jay nodded his agreement and the professor walked towards the door, turning to look back at the quadruped one more time.

Jay tapped the number into the lock pad, waited for the green light, then opened his apartment door. He'd put the quadruped in a cardboard box with packing straw which he slid onto the counter before fumbling for the light switch. The bright, efficient overheads illuminated a stark, white apartment. A kitchenette, small table, bathroom, a mattress and, aside from a few books on the floor by the bed, not much else. Jay didn't have much when he moved in and never felt the need to add to his belongings. No pictures, mementos, postcards on the fridge, no music. Jay was fine with the view from the large window and the noise of the city.

He slid his laptop out of his bag and fired it up, settling into the single dining chair while he waited. The blinking cursor waited for him on the top of the blank document. Jay stared back, hating that he had to do this. He stood to fetch the quadruped from the box and placed it on the table in front of him for inspiration. He struggled to decipher the expression on the face that he had made, he found it disquieting, like it was waiting for an answer from him. He stood again and walked over to the window.

Maybe a walk would get things flowing, a quick coffee at the bar down the street.

As soon as his feet hit the street in the golden light of the late afternoon he started to follow his long shadow along a familiar route. He willfully let his mind disengage, content to believe he was merely walking. He chose not to recognize that the streets were getting smaller and scruffier as he moved deeper into the North side of the city.

7

The sun had eventually come out and he began to feel its warmth soaking into him. He had woken sometime in the early hours to see the school kids had gone so he had stumbled off the gangplank to the terminal, bleary-eyed and confused. He'd hid out in the bathroom, keeping warm and wondering what to do. The terminal seemed to be miles from anywhere. Finally, he crept out, bought a muffin and a soda from the snack stand, then figured out he needed to spend the rest of his money on the shuttle train to the city.

That was hours and hours ago. Since then, he had been wandering aimlessly around the city, ducking out of sight whenever he saw a cop. He was wretched with anxiety over what to do. He could picture his mom worrying the Saint Christopher around her neck and chain-smoking, he could imagine Miss Klein walking the beach with Boop searching for clues, he found it hard to imagine Angela and he stopped imagining altogether when he thought about his dad. He couldn't go back, the places he wanted to go back to were no longer the same.

He was still cold and felt hungry again. He fingered the few coins in his pocket and realized he was probably not cut out to be a drifter. As he wandered down a side street, he came across on old-school diner. Not old and tacky, but properly old, with peppermint tiles and brass soda taps. It looked nice and it was pretty quiet, so he went inside.

He slid into an empty booth, enjoying the warmth and the soft seat. Almost immediately, a waitress glided up to the table, order pad in hand. Coby was expecting one of the stout, matronly ladies he had seen at the back. The athletic, young woman at his table had the whole frilly apron deal but that stopped abruptly at her bleached white crew cut that contrasted with her flawless, dark skin. She wore heavy, winged mascara and eyebrow piercings, her name tag read "Jaime".

"Hey, hon, can I start you with coffee or something while you look at the menu?"

She slapped a thick menu on the table and a big glass of water. Coby could tell she was scanning him up and down, quickly and efficiently like a cyborg.

"Nah, thanks, I'll just take a look at the menu. Thanks."

She clicked her pen a couple of times and gave him a raised-eyebrow smile that made her piercings move.

"I'll check right back."

She made him nervous and he stole a look back to the serving area to make sure she wasn't making a call. She was just laughing with the older servers. He flipped open the menu and looked to see if there was anything he could afford. There wasn't, but he fidgeted with the coins in his pocket hoping that something would reveal itself for seventy-eight cents. Jaime was suddenly back with her pen.

"Okay, hon, what will it be?

Coby furrowed his brow and tried to be nonchalant.

"You know, I think I'm good, I might come back later."
Jaime's smile dropped a bit to something more sincere.
"You hungry, dude?"

Coby nodded.

"You got any money?"

Coby shook his head, Jaime nodded slowly.

"What's your name, dude?"

"Coby."

"Well, Coby, I'm Jaime and my shift is just about done. We're allowed a piece of pie after work but I usually find it hard to finish. You wanna be fork buddies?"

"Sure, if you don't mind?"

"I don't."

Coby smiled and clumsily handed her the menu as she turned back to the kitchen. He relaxed a little and took some long gulps of the iced water. He suddenly saw himself reflected in the big mirror behind the booths. A pale, scruffy kid with curly, dark hair that was greasy and lop-sided, new zits around his nose, dark rings under his eyes. The red plaid jacket that obviously wasn't his. He was surprised when a sob welled up in his chest and caught in the back of his throat. He swallowed it down and blinked the tears out of his eyes when he saw Jaime coming up the aisle.

Jaime looked very different without the old-fashioned uniform. She wore a red fitted jacket over a black vee-neck shirt and skinny jeans. She looked very sophisticated and kind of dramatic. She swung a book bag into the booth with one hand and slid a slice of blueberry pie with whipped cream and two forks across to Coby with the other.

"Best in the city."

Coby took a polite forkful as he watched Jaime fire up a laptop and read through some underlined sections in a math textbook. The pie was delicious and he tried not to wolf it down.

He watched the regular people pass the diner windows. A few came in to pick up sweets for after dinner, the sun was going down. The idea of night made him shiver. He jumped a little when Jaime spoke.

"Coby, are you a runaway?"

Coby put down his fork and swallowed.

"No, I was just checking stuff out, but I lost my wallet."

Jaime looks up from her text book and straight into his eyes.

"If you are a runaway, bad things could happen to you."

Coby swallowed again and his throat trembled.

"What bad things?"

Jaime looked sad and opened her mouth to speak but then seemed to change her mind and sighed before continuing.

"When I was younger, things got messed up and I had to run away too. I came to the city and a few bad things did happen but this nice woman noticed me, and what was happening, and helped me out. If you need help, I can do the same for you."

Coby wonders what the bad things were and feels another sob building in his throat. He coughs to cover it then looks Jaime square in the eye.

"Yes, I'd like that, thank you."

Jaime smiled.

"Eat up, I've got class."

Jaime was going to community college because she wanted to be a nurse. She worked as a waitress and a babysitter, she wanted her own apartment so she could have a cat. She explained all of this as they walked through a pretty park in the warm, dusk air.

"I don't want you to freak out but you should come up with a new name for yourself, something easy to remember. If you give your real name they will contact your parents and send you home. Unless you want that, which would be fine."

"No, I can't do that."

"Okay, well, keep it simple like I said. Because you are so young with no ID, I'm going to have to vouch for you. So, let's be very clear. I'm going to help you get a place to stay and you are going to follow the shelter rules, go to school and stay away from drugs. I am not your mom, I'm just helping you out like that lady did for me. Are we clear?"

"Yes, for sure, I got it."

By now, they were standing outside a shabby, red brick building. Jaime walked up to the heavy red door under a security light and pressed the buzzer. A voice crackled through the intercom, Jaime said something about admissions and the door lock buzzed open.

The inside was shabby too with chipped paint and frayed carpets but it was warm and smelled of hearty food. Coby stood by Jaime and watched a mob of noisy kids spill down the stairs into the lobby then push through a swing door at the far end. Through the open door he could see cafeteria tables and a trolley with jugs of water and plastic cups. Sweeping along the stragglers was an older heavy-set man with wild white hair and matching eyebrows, wearing a baggy sweater with several holes showing the pink shirt beneath.

"Feeding time at the zoo!" The man shouted.

He laughed all the way over to them and shook both their hands with gusto.

"Henry Kim, director, welcome. Let's go to my office, find a little peace."

Henry Kim asked some questions while Coby played with a stress ball from the bowl full on the table. He tried out his new name, which felt weird, but said as little as he could and Henry Kim did not push him for more details. After a while, Henry Kim asked Coby to wait outside for a boy called Coop. As he leaned against the wall nervously waiting, he could hear Jaime and Henry Kim arguing about something but not in an angry way. A tall, kid with dreads and thick glasses came out of the cafeteria and walked over to him.

"You the new kid?"

Coby nodded.

"I'm Coop, let's get some chow."

Coby followed Coop into the dining room. There were about twenty kids, girls and boys, all around his age or a bit older. Coop handed him a tray and they joined the line of fidgeting kids waiting to serve themselves some pasta from a large pan. Coop nudged him.

"It looks nasty but it's good."

The rest of dinner was kind of a blur until Henry Kim appeared to show him to his room. He was sharing with Coop and two other boys. Henry Kim gave him a clean pair of old pajamas, a towel and a plastic baggie with toiletries, he went over some rules and said they would talk more in the morning. Jaime didn't come to say goodbye. Coby waited for his turn in the bathroom to brush his teeth and wash his face. He avoided looking at the kid in the mirror.

He heard but didn't listen to the quiet murmurs of the other boys until Henry Kim shouted down the corridor that it was lights out time. The room went dark and Coby wriggled deeper into the soft bed, allowing his deep tiredness to gather behind his closed eyes. And, just like that, he was someone else in a different place.

8

Jay pulled open the door of the grocery store and stepped inside. The girl was not behind the counter but he could hear the familiar murmur and click of the uncles. As he picked his way around bags of rice, he entered the smoky pool of light over the chess table. One of the bearded men deliberately leaned back in his chair and looked directly into Jay's eyes. The intense, black stare was unmistakably hostile so Jay did not even try to smile in greeting but dropped his gaze and hurried past.

The loading dock was stacked with cots and folded piles of rugs. Jay lifted his hand to knock on the door but it was already hanging open, so he pushed it back and started up the silent stairs.

The landing was much bigger than it had been as many of the cloth-partitioned cells had been deconstructed, including his. He started to walk around the floor looking for Valy when a flash of red caught his eye in the far corner. He moved closer to get a better look through the thin gap in the hanging cloth. The red-suited figure was sitting on the edge of a cot, his mitten-covered hands hanging from his knees and his head dropped low on his chest. All Jay could see of the face was the top of a domed forehead that was ghoulishly pale. The sound of steps on the stairs made the figure look up and Jay recoiled at the blank white mask, the chin lined with spines. Someone grabbed his arm and he spun around to face a panting Valy.

"Jay, man, you gotta call. Da fuck you doin' here?"

Valy did not look himself. He was sweaty and pale, his beard untrimmed and his usual pompadour in uncombed tufts. There were dark stains on the front of his white hoodie. He was glued to his phone screen, texting with his thumbs.

"Who is that weird guy back there?"

"There's no-one here, man, we shut it down."

Jay turned back to check the room in the corner and, like before, the figure had disappeared.

"What do you mean you shut it down?"

"I told you, my uncles want to do things different now."

Valy stopped furiously texting and looked up at Jay.

"Chill, chill, I'm gonna hook you up. Wait here."

Valy ducked into one of the rooms and came back with a cardboard box that he handed to Jay. Inside there was a lamp, some tools and the pipe Jay had made. Jay nodded as he understood what this meant. Valy reached into his pocket and brought out a small block of something wrapped in tinfoil.

"This is the new product, it's a lot purer, y'know, stronger, so be cool."

Jay took the tablet and reached for his wallet. Valy shook his head and put his hand out.

"Naw, man, this is on the house. Just get a phone so can we can liaise, yeah?"

Valy put his pinging phone away and started to unwind a rope that was wrapped around a cleat on the wall. Jay saw that the rope ran up to some pulley-blocks then spidered out to support the large frame for the partitions. Valy let the rope go and, like a magician's trick, the whole frame dropped from the ceiling to the floor. The large loft space was completely empty but for the dust motes in the air.

Jay hurried back to his apartment feeling haunted by the weirdness of his meeting with Valy. He found himself double-checking flashes of red clothing on the street and was relieved to reach the lobby of his building.

Safely inside his apartment, Jay slid the box onto the counter next to the box from the quadruped. Both boxes were the same, not just the same size but also with the same logo. Navy Cutter Rum, a cheap brand he remembered from the liquor cabinet as a kid. The thought led him to the freezer and a frosted bottle of Polish vodka. He reached in for the bottle then found a lone sake cup in the spartan cupboard beside the fridge. He poured a deep draft of the glycerine liquid, his fingers melting clear circles on the bottle.

When he slid into the chair his laptop woke up, revealing the blinking cursor still at the top of the blank document. Jay took a razor-cold swallow and waited for it to transform into a warm glow in his belly. He juggled words in his head, looking for an opening statement on which to hang the thread-bare, mediocre essay he could almost imagine writing. He looked over at the quadruped for inspiration but it just murmured to his ego with its fine lines and proud stance. Jay leaned back in his chair and reached for the bottle to refill his cup. He tried typing a dry, factual sentence, then another. Just as quickly his cup ran dry and he was increasingly aware of the foil-covered block in his pocket. He tapped in a couple of other words, deleted them and tried again. The deadline was midnight but the professor would probably not open it until the morning. Jay stood, refilled his cup, and walked over to the window. He rested his drink on the sill and looked out over the city, the Saturday night crowds an emulsion of flowing color in the streets below.

His laptop pinged, which it never did. He wandered back to the table, knocking back his drink. He dropped awkwardly into the chair, realizing he was feeling a little drunk. There was a green bubble from the school messaging system, the user was Lutkin62:

"Hi Jay, it looks like you took your submission piece home (your shelf is empty) but I need it for a panel assessment. I will also need the write-up we discussed by midnight. Thanks. Prof Lutkin."

Jay stared at the green bubble of text, hating it deeply. He thought back to their stifled conversation that afternoon. What did he call it, the tragedy? That heartbreaking call on the pay phone one rainy afternoon in the fall. The moment any remains of his childhood were crushed underfoot. The thick, buzzing silence in the empty hallway as he kept reassembling the words in an impossible puzzle.

Jay found his fingertips had been tracing the block in his pocket. He accepted that, on some level, he had already made a choice and submitted to it without further anguish. He closed the laptop and went over to the counter where Valy's box sat waiting. He didn't have a layout tray, so he put the items out on the coffee table by the small couch.

He laid out the pipe, the cutting and rolling tools, the needle, and then lit the oil lamp. He took the foil block from his pocket and opened it to reveal the sticky, black cube inside. Jay walked over to close the window blinds, then turned out all of the lights until the oil lamp was the only source of illumination. He settled on the couch in front of the paraphernalia and felt daunted. This was something Valy had always done for him, with his fluid, practiced motions. Jay had watched him dozens of times but realized this is why the lounge had been so important. However, the urge to slip out of life's brutal march for a moment was more than enough impetus to give it a try.

Jay cut a piece of the opium and started to heat and roll it as he had seen Valy do. Making a cleanly shaped pill was much harder than it looked, it seemed like he was using too much but found it hard to work a smaller amount. In the end , he gave up and used the needle to set what he had on the smoking bowl, reclined on the couch and tilted the bowl towards the heat of the lamp.

The first draw was so rough and acrid that Jay wondered if he had done something wrong, the smoke reeked of vinegar. The high came fast and hard but he felt good. The iris of his sensations opened and closed, dilating to an epic vista. He leaned into the lamp again and drew as hard as he could.

He was absolutely lost in a dark, roaring place. Something started to feel very wrong, he needed to pull himself up. It was so hard, dreaming you are awake but knowing you are asleep. Finally, finally, the sideways lamp swam into view. He tried to stand but tumbled across the table and watched his beautiful pipe shatter as he followed it to the floor. His chest hurt, the light started to flicker. The door at the end of the hallway seemed so far away. His eyes kept closing and he kept forcing them open.

The light dipped to almost darkness, then flared again behind him. In its glow, he saw the red-suited figure step into the hallway. Where had it been hiding? It walked slowly towards him, then lowered it's face down to his. Jay could see it clearly now, he could see that the mask was the white shell of a horseshoe crab. The crab's eyes approximating those of the wearer, the spines and tail telson creating a villain's beard. An urgent trill was rising in his ears. The figure brought up a black-mittened hand and started to lift the mask. An oily, black wave towered up and crushed Jay deep down into an icy trench where breath was a memory.

9

Coby thought the screen printing was really neat. Miss Klein showed him how to simplify his cover design to just blocks of color. The first pass was only chunks and lines of red on white paper that didn't really look like anything, but when they did the black on top, pow! The doll and the logo just popped out of the white background like magic. It seemed like Miss Klein was pretty impressed and Angela wanted one of the shirts, which felt good.

As they cleaned up, Angela looked at Coby with a head-tilt that meant he should follow along.

"Hey, mom, is it okay if me and Coby go down to the beach?"

Miss Klein didn't even look up from the utility sink as she scrubbed a screen with her brush.

"Sure, guys, but home by four for both of you please."

"Thanks, mom."

Angela dunked her wet paper towel in the trash can and then chased Coby's back with wiggly fingers to get him out of the room as quickly as possible. She took the white pony from the table as they passed, nuzzling it under her arm. Coby liked that she was not embarrassed to enjoy something childish like that.

They ran down the path through the dunes but both stopped at the crest overlooking the bay. The soft light of the late afternoon gilded the slick, curling breakers as they crept up the wide beach with the rising tide. It was perfect.

"So, where is this secret place?"

"Far end."

They both did their trademark, superhero-run down the steep dune path, trying to fly between footfalls. In the past they would have both lost out to gravity and tumbled, giggling down the last slope but now their stronger bodies let them run it out and jog to the beach.

In the quiet, as they caught their breaths, Coby felt a different energy between them, he was very aware of when her body brushed close to his. The sand was beginning to give way to the splintered rock strata at the far end of the beach. The hull of the wreck was a shimmering orange in the escaping heat of the afternoon. Angela turned to him with an outstretched palm.

"So?"

"Over there."

As they walked up to the wreck, Angela's expression changed.

"Mom said I shouldn't go in there."

"No, it's totally fine once you know how to do it. Trust me."

Coby showed her how to grip the edge of the gunwale and put her foot in the porthole, then held the pony for her as he helped pull her up. As she dropped onto the deck, Coby steadied her with a hand on her side. When she straightened, her face was very close to his and glowing in the low, golden sun. He could see the faint down on her freckled cheeks and the gold-dusted, emerald strands of her irises. She leaned in to him, just slightly, and he stopped breathing. He knew he was supposed to do something, like on TV, but he didn't know how it worked. He decided he would just pretend he hadn't noticed.

"The steps are slippy and the bottom one is missing, so be careful."

Angela leaned back and nodded, she seemed disappointed which made him feel kind of happy, a double-dip. He went first to show her where to step and they were soon in his cave.

The heat of the day and the near-kiss nervousness had made Coby start to sweat, so he took off his coat and draped it around the remains of the stair rail. Angela was nervously glancing around the belly of the trawler.

"This place is super-creepy."

"Are you kidding? It's so cool, like from a movie."

"A horror movie."

They both laughed and things felt more normal again. Then Coby heard the scratchy rumble of Kabu awakening. Much more quickly than usual, his white form drifted out of the shadows in the pool.

Kabu was very excited to see Angela and started to demand Coby take him to her. Coby wasn't sure but Kabu insisted, over and over. He turned to Angela.

"The boat isn't the secret, are you ready?"

"I guess."

"Close your eyes."

Angela closed her eyes, swaying slightly as she clutched her pony. A bemused smile crept onto her lips and she used one hand to brush the hair from the sides of her face. The feeling Coby had during the near-kiss briefly resurfaced but he pushed it away.

Kabu was waiting in the shallow end and Coby reached in to carefully push his fingers into the sand under the edge of his shell. Coby had never picked up Kabu and was surprised by the weight as he came out of the water. Seawater soaked into his shirt and jeans as he lifted the crab over the side of the tank and started to walk softly towards Angela.

Kabu was imploring Coby to bring him closer and closer, so Coby lifted the crab to be in front of Angela's face. Kabu's pale legs were clawing out from under his shell, searching for purchase.

Sensing that Coby was close, Angela leaned in a little closer as she had done on the deck.

"Okay, open your eyes."
Angela's eyes opened almost sleepily at first, then exploded open in horror. She screamed and shoved Coby away, driving a strong arm into his shoulder. Coby stumbled on a weed-covered rock and dropped the heavy crab, which landed upside down on a corroded metal rib with a sickening crunch.

Angela was crying and shouting about something. Coby ignored her and ran to Kabu who had fallen completely silent. He lifted the crab and turned it over, sky-blue blood ran over his hands from the deep split in the shell. A deep rage that he hadn't felt since the trouble at school started to vibrate and expand in his chest. He gently laid the motionless crab on the sand and stood to face

Angela. She was whimpering and clutching her pony, a bead of snot was running down her lip.

Allowing all expression to drop from his face, Coby walked over to her and tried to take the pony from her hands. He was shocked by her strength as they wrestled over the sculpture but she lost her grip and it was her turn to stumble. Unable to get a foot down behind her, she fell backwards into the bulkhead, striking it with a deep, metallic thud and slipping to the floor. During the tussle, the pony had fallen between them and landed, undamaged, on the same large, sandy area where Kabu lay.

Angela lifted a hand weakly towards the pony, her voice almost inaudible.

"Please."

Coby's rage filled his mind and his muscles as he glowered at the perfect pony in the sand. There was a rusted-off section of railing laying in the sand, covered with weed and barnacles. Coby pried it out of the sand, enjoying the coarse weight in his hand. He walked over to the pony, looked directly at Angela, then brought the metal rod down as hard as he could, shattering the pony into tiny fragments.

Angela didn't say anything. She was holding the back of her head with one hand, the other lay loosely in her lap. She seemed to be staring sadly at the shards of her pony but her eyes were glassy and unfocused, like she was daydreaming.

Coby heard a faint voice, he couldn't tell if it was Kabu or Angela over the sound of the waves but it told him to go. He dropped the bar and scrambled up the steps to the deck then jumped the gunwale to land on the flat rocks below.

The wind had picked up, whipping the climbing breakers to thunder and hiss against the beach. The anger drained out of him, leaving him feeling hollow and tired as he trudged over the deep sand. His hands were sticky with the drying blood.

PART 2

10

The feeling was familiar, drifting up through a liminal column from one place to another, yet this felt very different. The deep, dark place he had left still snatched at him, the ascent seemed endless and exhausting and for once the surface promised relief.

Jay allowed his eyes to squint open. The room was very bright, white and small, he figured he was in his apartment. He looked to the foot of his bed and saw a blurry, hunched figure in a red jacket. He panicked and forced his eyes to focus, blinking furiously. It was Coby, staring at him with shock that split into a smile. Jay pushed himself up to speak, which came out as a croak.

"What are you doing here?"

"Are you kidding me? I saved you! I let myself in with the code and you were just lying on the floor. You weren't breathing and the couch was on fire."

"On fire?"

"Yeah, I thought you were dead."

"Where am I?"

"The hospital, duh."

All of these facts floated around in Jay's mind as he lay back on the pillow but they refused to fit together. The door to his room swung open and a tall doctor strode in with a chart in her hands.

"So, how are we feeling this afternoon?"

She was in her fifties and looked South Asian but her accent had the unmistakable guttural clip of the city.

"I'm feeling okay, thanks."

"Well, I'm surprised. If you were a cat you'd be nervous about how few lives you had left."

She looked up from the chart to give him a piercing look that he felt was both an admonishment and a professional assessment. She looked back to the chart and flipped back a few pages.

"The EMTs entered your apartment after the fire alarm was tripped and smoke was reported. You were unresponsive on the floor and barely breathing. You had low blood pressure, slow heart rate and hypoxia, so they administered naloxone and brought you to ER. Your vitals were difficult to stabilize and, frankly, it was touch and go for a while."

Jay realized he had no memory of any of this but that last comment chilled him.

"You mean, I nearly died?"

"Well, you certainly didn't leave much wriggle room."

Jay was suddenly aware of the wires running from his body to the equipment by his bed. The doctor seemed frustrated.

"Thank you for taking care of me."

"You are welcome, but let me say this. Aside from the smoke inhalation, you tested positive for opioids and alcohol, and black-tar heroin was noted at the scene. Your behavior was doing its best to kill you."

Jay couldn't look at Coby, he felt ashamed and wretched that he had to hear this. The doctor closed the chart and sank into her right hip, sighing through her nose. Her voice was softer as she continued.

"You were lucky this time but I don't want to see you back here. I'm going to leave you some material about opioid addiction and rehab, we have some great programs here, please read them. And remember that cat, young man."

She punctuated the end of her speech with a deep look from her dark eyes directly into his. She didn't waver until he nodded meekly.

"Good. The nurse will be in to draw some blood for a couple more tests then, if everything looks fine, you will be discharged later this afternoon."

With that she left. The gravity of the doctor's words were beginning to sink in and he made himself look at Coby. He was quietly looking out of the rain-streaked window, there were little creases of worry on his forehead but he seemed clean and fed.

"Hey, that's my jacket."

Coby looked down at the baggy plaid jacket and played with a button.

"You want it back?"

"Nah, it looks better on you."

Coby smiled and hopped off the window sill.

"I could go for some pizza."

Jay realized that he could go for some pizza too.

It took a couple of hours to get out of the hospital and they went straight to a hole-in-the-wall pizza joint and got some sodas and a large plain to go. Jay borrowed some scissors from the waitress to cut the identity band off his wrist.

The rain had passed and the afternoon had become fresh and sunny. Coby wanted to go down by the river, so they found an empty bench set back from the riverwalk and put the pizza box between them. The salivary glands in Jay's mouth prickled as he bit into the end of his folded slice, he hadn't been this hungry in a long time and the pizza was perfect. Coby was chewing enthusiastically too, so they sat in silence and watched the river.

Jay rarely came here and wondered why. The weeping willows trailed their leaves in the water that ran under the elegant arc of the granite bridge, it was very peaceful. Directly opposite there was a large marble sculpture, something modern partially hidden by the trees, Jay hadn't even noticed it before.

When they had both eaten enough, Jay closed the box and leaned back on the bench. Coby was absently swirling the remains of his soda in the bottom of the can.

"So, Coby, how have you been?"

"Better than you, obviously."

The smile died on Jay's lips but he knew he deserved it.

"I'm sorry, I'm sure that was a scary experience."

"You never even thanked me. You thanked that doctor but you didn't thank me."

Coby eyes were welling up and his bottom jaw started to tremble.

"Coby, I really am sorry and, yes, of course, thank you. You did save me, you saved my life."

"Asshole."

Coby's fists were clenched and Jay let the insult wash over him, absorbing it, letting it dissipate. He waited until

Coby softened, let him choose to speak when he was ready.

"It's okay. How I've been, it's okay."

"Good, you look well."

"Henry Kim is cool, he's a nice guy. Food looks gross but it's amazingly pretty good. I've been hanging out with Kyle and Coop a lot, he's crazy, we play hoops after school."

"So, yeah, how's school?"

"It sucks. And that food looks ok but is totally gross. Social studies is okay and I like art. The other kids know we come from the shelter so they make fun of us, those assholes with three hundred dollar sneakers and fancy phones. My grades are good though."

"I'm proud of you, dude. What grade are you in now?"

Coby's eyebrows bob up in frustration.

"I'm in seventh grade, for the whole year."

"Wow, nearly in high school."

"Yeah, high school."

Coby doesn't look happy about this thought but straightens up and runs a hand through his curls.

"Then Jaime is going to help me get into the community college. I'm going to get a cool job too so I can get my own place. I'm going to get a dog."

"Wow, man, you have it all figured out, that's awesome."

Coby nodded but his smile quickly faded. Jay picked up the pizza box and stood up.

"Let's head back to my place, we can take the riverwalk."

Coby yawned and stood up too, seemingly happy with the plan.

Whatever they had given him at the hospital was wearing off and Jay was filled with an aching fatigue that brought with it a sense of despair. He knew it was time to take stock and make changes in his life, there was still time. His thoughts were interrupted by a figure emerging from a stand of bushes by the river. What Jay had feared was a menacing, white face was just a balloon printed with a radio station logo, held by a young boy in a red tracksuit. He exhaled with relief but his mind kept returning to splinters of the red-suited figure, like a tongue probing a throbbing tooth.

He caught up with Coby and they walked side-by-side down the concrete pathway, stepping aside to let a determined jogger with a running stroller filled with miserable twins rumble past.

As they entered the shadow of the bridge, Jay was aware of several shadowy figures shuffling around cardboard boxes and shopping carts loaded with filled trash bags. He walked over to one, an older lady in a wooly hat, and offered her the leftover pizza. She took it with rough hands and smiled with ruined teeth.

"Bless you, hon."

Coby turned around with an irritated scowl.

"Why did you do that?"

"Because she might be hungry, dude."

"I might be hungry later and I'm not a fucking low-life, junkie!"

Coby strode on ahead. Again, Jay let the jab run through him, mitigating it through his whole body. He turned to give an apology to the woman but she was already sharing out the slices with the dark forms behind her.

Jay walked at his own pace, giving Coby his space. After a while, the path split and one arm rode up the embankment to another bridge. Jay could see that Coby was leaning on the bridge wall looking down into the river. Jay came up beside him and rested his forearms on the wall. Coby didn't say anything for a few moments then turned to Jay.

"We have to find Angela."

He was calm, and his eyes were focused on Jay's. Jay blinked before he did.

"You think she's here?"

"Isn't this where everyone comes? The city?"

"Okay. Let's find Angela."

11

It is difficult to remember the time when I was a man. I know I still ache for the pleasures of touch and taste. What pleasures they were and what a man I was. A gifted, handsome warrior from a powerful family that was feared by so many, which pleased me.

As a young man, I had grown to very much enjoy the the thrills of tsujigiri, expertly concealing myself by a quiet roadside until a hapless peasant shuffled within reach of my cruelest blade. Usually, I would simply remove their surprised head from their shoulders but sometimes I took the time to practice my sword work. If they screamed and died without honor, I would make the extra effort to discover their family members and add them to my tally as well. This tally became my obsession and, eventually, my downfall. I wished to be the first to take a thousand lives and gain spiritual invincibility. I was very close to my goal but my efforts had caused the peasants to become wary and avoid walking the roads alone.

Frustrated by the lack of a quarry, I rode deep into the North to areas I did not know and where, I reasoned, I would also be unknown. I came across a well-worn path at the edge of a rocky bay, just as the sun was setting and illuminating the sea mist over the water. It was a place of remarkable beauty. A cleft in some rocks provided a perfect vantage point so I hid myself there and became as silent as the rocks around me.

I did not have to wait long before I saw a hunched figure emerge from the thickening mist. Dressed in a wide hat and straw raincoat, the figure had a fisherman's pole on one shoulder. The fading, murky light prevented me from seeing the features or even sex of the peasant but the slow, bent gait indicated a person of some age.

My heart started to beat quickly with the promise of what would soon come, that perfect agony of holding a thirst sure to be slaked. I decided that I would take my time with this one.

As the figure drew close, I dropped from the crevice in a silent, fluid movement, my katana already poised to slash the figure's chest. I stifled a smile as I waited to see the look of terror on the elderly face but with a movement that was shockingly fast and powerful, the figure swung its wooden fishing pole to knock the sword from my hand with such force it crushed my fingers.

I watched my perfect blade spin and drop into the water of the bay. My broken fingers screamed in pain and a deep vibration began to build in my chest. I turned my rage to the stooped figure in front of me. The figure slowly tilted up the brim of its hat to reveal its face. Not the toothless, wrinkled visage of an old fool but a featureless white face with impossibly deep set eyes that glowed amber from their black sockets.

I knew better than to battle such a spirit and spun away to retreat quickly into the forest. I had yet to take a single step when a pair of sharp, black talons gripped my arms like steel and the evil yokai began to drag me backwards towards the shore. I struggled and cursed but I could not weaken its fearsome hold and I soon felt the cold waters of the sea rise up my legs. With unrelenting strength, the yokai pulled me under the surface and deeper into the dark water. When I could fight no more, I watched the silvery globes of my final breath rise to the last of the sunlight.

When I was next aware in the deep, silent cold, I was filled with horror at what I had become. Trapped in an ugly, prehistoric shell, my body squat and unyielding, my senses so dull and simplistic. I realized with bitterness that the yokai's punishment was not without wit. As a child, I was taught to return any heikegani to the water with great respect if we happened upon one of those sacred crabs amongst the rocks on the shore. These crabs held the spirit of fallen Heike warriors, shown by the noble face of the warrior in the back shell of the crab. The yokai had trapped my spirit in this crude, pale abomination, giving a handsome warrior the face of an ugly crab.

Full of misery I wandered the vast deserts of the ocean floor for many years, struggling to accept my ignoble fate. I found I could easily will away the simple-minded sharks and the turtles that eyed me for food, while I had to dine on the dank, briny effluvia of the sea bed. I could feel pain but I felt I never aged and I felt no more urge to mate with a crab than I had as a human. I lived the life of an ugly, poor spinster until a wonderful thing happened.

I became aware of a deep, discordant vibration, like the one I had felt in my chest as a man, but this invaded my senses from without. Like a long blade drawn with a horsehair bow, the vibration filled me with emotions I had not felt in a long time. It grew in intensity until my primitive eyes made out the form of a naked young woman swimming towards me with a knife. The ama discarded a few empty shells then seemed puzzled when she spotted me. The next moment, I was picked up and helpless to escape as she followed the rope on her waist to the surface with powerful kicks from her muscular legs. I was dropped into a floating wooden tub with a few other simple creatures and she pushed us towards a small, shabby boat. With a practiced, single motion she pulled herself over the side and sat in the bow, wet and glistening in the golden sunlight. Long-forgotten pleasures ached within me as I drank in her beauty.

She placed the tub on the deck and looked over to an older man who was slumped in the stern of the dirty boat. The man was also dirty, his clothing streaked with stains and his greasy jowls were noisily suckling on a large earthenware jug. His rheumy eyes were regarding the girl with both hatred and lust, I could feel those frequencies pulsing and fighting each other within the man. The girl, naked and vulnerable under his gaze, was cleaning barnacles from an oyster shell with her knife. Her vibrations were joining the fugue, softer but with a sharp edge like the knife that felt good in her hands.

On very unsteady legs, the man rocked his way across the deck to the girl and looked into the tub with a sneer. He pointed at me and accused the girl of wasting his time. I did not care for this insolent drunkard. The girl shielded her eyes against the sun as she looked up to him towering over her. His hands shot out to grab her arms in a way that reminded me of the yokai and I could see the pattern of his grip was repeated in bruises all over the girl's thin arms.

The rising vibrations began to fill my body and it was sublime. I focused on the girl and the knife in her hand. I found power in the terrible resonance between them and willed the girl to do that which she secretly craved. When the man released her arm to raise his hand over her, I felt the chaotic vibration dilate to a single high pitch as she drove the blade up under his sternum, her strong shoulders plunging it to the very hilt. I felt a deep flood of pleasure that I had not known since the tsujigiri. It filled my senses until I felt myself floating out of my ugly body. I watched the drunkard, the knife still in his chest, slip backwards over the side of the boat. I saw the girl lean over the stern and wash the blood from her hands and breasts. I saw her drop my living body into the sea, yet I remained, hovering over the boat like an invisible gull.

I followed the girl as she rowed towards shore, feeling her frequency thrum. The rage and killing filled me with the power to escape my dull, primitive cage and move upon the land once more.

Once the girl had pulled her boat ashore, I drifted through the crude, little fishing village feeding on the anguish of widows and causing bloody fights between the men drinking in the izakaya. Some grew fearful and whimpered when I approached and I wondered how I must appear to them but most were oblivious as I slipped into their spirit and used their animal.

It was glorious to feel so much fire again but as the villagers became sober and quiet I felt my my influence wane. In time, I had a sense of dissipating like morning mist beneath a hot sun and a gentle pull at my back that continued to grow in intensity. Without warning the pull hardened and I was once again being dragged backwards into the sea. I fought against the invisible force with all my might but had to watch the bright colors of the land recede from my sight as I was plunged deep into the water.

When I next became aware, I was back in the cursed, white crab. My senses dull and my fleeting pleasures now just memories.

This was how it was to be. Between yawning stretches of time, unwitting fishermen would bring me aboard their vessel. Tightly coiled with frustration, I would immediately set to work, relentlessly seeding dark thoughts and mistruths in the minds of the crew. Fanning the embers of dissatisfaction that were already there, until fires burned behind all of their eyes. I built those ragged frequencies into a roaring cacophony, turning knife fights into mutiny and sabotage into murder.

When blood was spilled and lives were taken, I could rise again. I would attach myself to the darkest of the survivors, have him return my ugly body to the safety of the deep, then follow him to the complex, violent creatures of the land. There, I would feed my senses amongst the brothels and bars, the broken and the weak. I gorged as much as I could, never able to completely sate my hunger.

Inevitably, with time my power would ebb away and I would be dragged back to the sea. I came to accept this and I would lie in wait like my days of tsujigiri. I came to accept that I myself had become a yokai and it pleased me.

12

Coby pushed ahead as they walked down the corridor towards Jay's apartment and ran to the door to punch in the code. Jay considered asking him to wait but knew he was just putting off the inevitable. Coby shoved through the door as Jay reached it, which irritated him, as did the eviction notice taped to his door. Inside, Coby laughed.

"This place is fucking trashed."

Jay forced himself to enter, ignoring the stern-looking envelopes on the mat and closing the door behind him. It was indeed fucking trashed. The badly charred couch was covered with fire retardant powder and soaked with oil from the broken lamp. Long streaks of soot fingered up the wall to the ceiling. Coby crunched across the shards of the broken pipe and pieces of paraphernalia on the floor, the overturned vodka bottle lay in its own viscous pool. Jay sighed and allowed the shame to flood through him afresh.

Coby walked over to Jay's laptop and tapped on the space bar, which also irritated Jay.

"Looks like you have a shit ton of messages."

Jay moved closer to the screen and opened the message app, they were all from Professor Lutkin. His mind spun through the usual gallery of choices, looking for escape. He was surprised to find he no longer cared to run.

He left Coby to mess with the laptop and went over to the dusty, push-button phone on the kitchen counter. He tapped in the number at the bottom of the professor's signature. It rang only once.

"Professor Lutkin speaking."

"Hi Professor, this is Jay."

"Jay! Well, this is, uh, a surprise."

"I saw you had left a lot of messages, I wanted to call and apologize."

The professor was silent for a moment.

"It's okay, Jay, I heard what happened through the housing office. How are you feeling?"

"I'm doing okay."

"Good, good. I was worried about you."

The professor's voice cracked a little on the final word. Jay realized that the bitterness he had felt towards this man was childish and ungrateful. His own voice was a little thick as he continued.

"Thanks, but I'm fine. I just wanted to see what I should be doing."

The professor let out a wavering sigh.

"Yes, right. Well, I'm afraid the scholarship has been retracted, no latitude there. However, I did speak with the dean on your behalf and she agreed that you can continue with the course on the condition that you maintain a passing grade and attend the program at the Campus Recovery Center. Does that seem reasonable?"

"Yes, of course, thank you."

"Well, great. I explained the situation to the head of the housing office and I think if you were able to fix the damage and give him a sincere apology, I have a feeling that he will forget about that eviction notice."

"Thank you, professor, I will. Thank you for helping me."

The waver came back into the professor's voice as he replied.

"It's no problem, really, we are family here, right? Come into my office when you are feeling better in a couple of days."

"Sounds good, thanks again."

"Bye, Jay."

"Bye."

Jay felt ragged and threadbare but he also felt somehow lighter as he replaced the receiver. He looked over at Coby who was scowling at him, the blue glow of the laptop screen adding to the ugliness of his expression.

"Why don't you get a real phone, you fucking suck-up?"

"I don't want to. Why don't you stop swearing at me?"

"I was just kidding."

"Kidding like dad?"

Coby shot him a dark, flinty look then slowly shook his head and closed the laptop screen. He noticed the quadruped sitting on the table and suddenly looked like a kid again as his dour sneer gave way to open-mouthed surprise.

"Did you make that?"

"Yeah, do you like it?"

"It's awesome! Can I have it?"

Jay looked at the sculpture and wondered why that lump of clay had transfixed him for so long.

"Sure, just be careful, it's really delicate and I still need to take it into school."

Coby gently lifted the quadruped and turned it under the light.

"It's like you can almost see through it."

Jay opened the door to the cleaning cupboard in the corner of the kitchen. He took out a broom and some trash-bags and shook them at Coby.

"Wanna help?"

Coby lowered the quadruped and looked at Jay with a serious expression.

"Wait, we gotta look for Angela first. You promised."

Jay tried to look neutral as he leaned the broom against the wall.

"Okay, so do you have some kind of plan for that?"

"We post a missing person thing on the city free ads with your lame laptop."

"Don't we need a picture?"

Coby reached into the back pocket of his jeans and pulled out a creased photo that he handed to Jay.

"It's maybe my favorite."

Jay flattened the curled corners and smiled at the photo of the curly-haired girl, it was a great picture.

"Don't we need to scan this?"

"You have a lame camera built into your lame laptop."

Jay used to know this stuff, how had he become so out of touch? He handed the photo back to Coby and used the broom to start cleaning up while Coby tapped away on the keyboard. It felt nice, them both quietly working on their tasks. Coby asked for the landline number and rolled his eyes, Jay just smiled and read it off the sticker on the phone.

After Jay swept up the debris and bagged it, he set about mopping the grimy tile flooring. There were a lot of dirty footprints from the fire, he recognized his own sneakers and some heavy work-boot treads that he assumed had come from the firemen or EMTs. Then he noticed some very odd looking prints that led from the bathroom and up the hall to the living area. They were vaguely comma-shaped, round at the front with a pointed heel and their texture was that of coarse-knit wool. There was only one set of these prints and, unlike the others, only traveled in one direction. Jay thought about the red-suited figure and felt his scalp prickle. He quickly slopped the hot sudsy water on the floor and mopped vigorously at the dried prints until the tile was clean.

After Jay had scrubbed the soot from the walls, he and Coby dragged the burnt couch down to the dumpster at the back of the building. It was a lot heavier than he remembered and Coby complained a lot. It felt good to walk back into the clean apartment with the late afternoon sun streaming through the window. Coby made straight for the fridge and snorted derisively when he opened the door.

"Why am I surprised your fridge is empty?"

The words seemed playful but Jay was aware of the judgment just below the surface. He deserved it, he accepted that, but it was making it hard to stay positive. Each jab made him aware of a quiet, keen longing that sent his mind back to the lounge, then to remember all that had happened and his promise to himself to take a different path. They needed to take care of one another.

Coby dropped into a dining chair and cradled the quadruped in his lap.

"I'm sorry, we can go down to the plaza. What do you to eat?"

"Pizza."

"Why am I surprised you said that? But that's cool, maybe add a side salad to keep those zits at bay."

Coby lifted a finger to the pocked skin on his chin and a flash of anger darkened his eyes.

"I meant both of us. You may have noticed I haven't exactly been a health nut recently."

Coby's expression softened but a sadness lingered.

"So, Coby, I've been thinking. I'm going to need to get a new couch and maybe I should get a sleeper."

"Fascinating."

"Well, if I don't get thrown out of here, I was thinking that you could use it and stay here instead of the shelter."

Coby looked up at Jay, his right leg beginning to jiggle on the floor.

"You serious?"

"Yeah. We can talk to Henry Kim, I'm sure it will be okay."

Coby looked around the apartment, seeing it differently, imagining it being his new home. Jay smiled, enjoying the moment.

Before Coby could say anything, the phone rang. Jay couldn't remember ever having heard the awful shrill tone and hoped it wasn't the housing office. He lifted the receiver.

"Hello?"

The reedy voice of an older man answered.

"Yes, good evening. I'm calling about your missing persons posting."

"Ah, yes, right. So, do you know where Angela is?"

Coby's head snapped up and he shot across the kitchen to stand by Jay, his balled fists clenched to his chest. Jay held the receiver between them.

"Not at this moment, but I can help you. Let me explain. My name is William Crump, I am a remote viewer and I would like to extend my services to you at this difficult time."

Jay rolled his eyes but Coby nodded encouragement, so Jay pushed on.

"I'm sorry, what exactly is a remote viewer?"

"Well, to put it simply, I have the ability to find hidden targets at a distance using extrasensory perception."

"Like a psychic?"

"Not exactly but I do employ the power of my mind."

"Right. And I'm guessing we would need to pay you for this service?"

"Only if I am successful, which I am sixteen percent of the time, so the odds are rather stacked in your favor financially. However, sixteen percent is considerably more than zero if you are hoping to find this person. We can discuss my fee when we meet."

Jay frowned and shook his head but Coby was pleading with prayer-hands and wide eyes. Jay relented.

"Okay, mister Crump, where would we be meeting you?"

"William, please. We can meet at my office at 10:00 am, if you have a pen I will give you the address."

Jay pointed to a drawer in the kitchen cabinets and Coby took out a pen and a napkin.

"If you can bring the original print of the photo in your ad that would be most useful and, please, no cologne, gum or music players when you come to the office."

He watched Coby chew his lip as he carefully printed the address on the napkin, then Jay said goodbye and hung up the phone. He became aware that as he fixed certain parts of his life others were coming adrift in the darkness behind him.

13

Much of my mortal life is difficult to remember, little moments sparking like sun-caught dust in a darkened room. However, one memory lingers that still gives me pleasure when I turn it over in my mind. She was a young peasant girl, a seamstress and quite beautiful. I had noticed her several times in the market and learned that she always left by the same road.

One evening, I took my chances and waited at the far end of a covered bridge on the same road. After a few false alarms with several old crones and a farmer, I was thrilled to see the girl enter the bridge. As she crested the apex of the bridge's arch, she turned to look down the river into the muted evening sun. She paused for a moment and allowed herself a tiny smile. The effect was intoxicating, such rare, flawless beauty.

As she approached, I stepped out and honored her grace by swiftly piercing her belly with my katana, barely drawing a drop of blood. She let out a sweet, little sigh and I was enraptured. She began to pull on the blade, slicing her fingers, the blood running from her elbows. I took my wakizashi in my free hand and plunged it into her left eye. She did not make another sound but started to shake on my blades. I slowly breathed in the moment then gently turned both blades in opposite directions, feeling the wakizashi grate in her eye socket. I looked deep into her right eye as she convulsed before the brightness finally left it. This memory is a like a candle in the deep, black ocean.

My memories as a yokai are different. They exist in overlapping waves between vast voids of barrenness. They are wonderful orgies of sensations but they fall away without ever reaching the exquisite sharpness of the tsujigiri killings. That said, my most recent experience took me through a torii to a new world of possibility, a gateway that would lead to soaring summits but also a profoundly hopeless dungeon.

I had learned to skirt the shallows of the shore where contact was more likely and, after a pitifully long famine, I sensed the approaching vibrations of men. Two approached, wading in the shallow water, and I did not struggle as I was lifted from the sandy bed and placed in a small, metal boat. The men seemed impressed by my appearance but when I regarded my squat, ugly relatives beside me in the boat, I was reminded that my physical form was devoid of all grace.

The men were meek and bland, so I decided to bide my time and see what else would present itself. After a short while, they hauled themselves into the boat and started moving towards a much bigger vessel that was at anchor a short distance offshore. As we got nearer, I was thrilled to sense the different frequencies of others and prepared myself for the sport ahead.

The men tied off the small boat at the stern of the bigger vessel and I felt myself being lifted onto deck. These were not coarse fisherman, I was handled gently and relieved I had no broken legs to regenerate. From the deck I was moved to a long room inside the boat, with metal benches running down the center and rows of deep troughs. One of the gentle, meek men placed me in a trough and began to carefully clean my shell, scraping off barnacles and weed. It was extraordinary to be touched like this after so long and it sparked a misty memory of a debauched afternoon in a disreputable bath-house. I was distracted by the discord of frequencies growing around me, it seemed a tension was building on old grievances.

I was placed on the bench and sensed a change in the atmosphere. A door opened and a large man walked into the room. I felt the other crew shrink away from him, his frequencies were a deep, pounding throb. He clapped his hands once then motioned a finger along the benches, his jaw clenching. Other crewmen approached and busied themselves around the central table. The large man picked me up in powerful hands and tossed me around as he examined my body. I felt indignant anger rise in my core and when my primitive eyes met his for a second, I looked deep into his spirit. His rage festered and boiled, he had hatred for all those around him. I thrilled imagining how I would use his animal.

Without warning, he roughly pushed me into some kind of frame and folded my body in half below the carapace. He strapped me down tightly then plunged a needle into the soft space between my shell plates. It enraged me to be trapped this way and forced to watch my own blood flow into glass bottle. I tried to focus on controlling the man's thundering frequencies but they constantly wove and dodged my efforts.

A wiry, dark-skinned man with bulging eyes, dressed in the livery of a captain, descended a staircase from the upper deck. He strode over to the large man and I felt both of their energies swell and tangle. The captain was worried about a strong storm that was quickly approaching and wanted to head back to the harbor, the large man cared only for quotas and pay-out. The two men entered a stand-off but the simmering aura of the large man bested the harried skipper. The captain muttered something about 'twenty-minutes', then strode back to the stairs.

A young woman approached the large man, quietly reasoning that the captain was responsible for their safety and the safety of the boat. She was quickly answered with a quivering finger to the face. There was so much to harvest but my focus wandered as the blood flowed out of my physical body. There was a shout and a shove, the frequencies of the large man were howling like the gale on a mountain peak.

I tried to gather myself as the men worked quietly on the rows of bleeding crabs, sensing their anxiety about the time it took to fill their bottles with the sky blue fluid. A sudden gust of wind rocked the boat, followed by the sizzle of hard rain against the portholes and a deep grumble of thunder. The large man spread his hands on the bench and swept his gaze around the room. All of the crew shrunk from his glare as lightning fractured the sky. The wind started to howl over the railings and whitecaps beat on the hull.

The large man removed the needle and efficiently released me from the strap. Free again I sharpened my senses and crept into his internal chaos. He walked over to a large empty tank at the stern end of the room and dropped me into the water. I threaded my way into his thoughts, trying to crystallize them into something I could use. The man lifted a boathook from a rack on the bulkhead and announced he was going to secure the dinghy so they could head over to the next area. The silence of the room was broken by the footfalls of the captain on the stairway. The large man growled and walked over to confront him. The captain announced the twenty minutes had elapsed and they were going back to harbor, he added that the large man and his workers would need to finish up immediately.

The large man snapped and I gleefully rode the tsunami of rage as he roared at the captain. The captain tried to stand his ground but he looked anxious then reached behind his back to draw a handgun on the large man. The large man fell silent, the captain's hand shook as it held the gun and the large man smirked. I blew encouragement into his thoughts like air on an ember. With a speed that belied his size, the large man swung the boathook, smashing the gun from the captain's hand. The captain fell to his knees, trying to reach the gun with his uninjured hand but the large man used both powerful arms to drive the metal tip of the boathook into the back of the captain's skull with a wet crunch. The captain slowly collapsed over his knees, blood flowing freely onto the white metal deck.

I felt my essential being lift out of the tank, engorged with howling black vibrations. I took the large man's spirit in my hands and forced him to look at the ring of silent crewman who were staring at him in horror, steadying themselves against the heaving of the boat. They are witnesses, I whispered in his core, everyone is a witness. That was all it took.

The large man snatched up the pistol, enjoying the familiar heft of the weapon, and used it to wave the crewmen through the hatchway onto the deck at the stern. The boat was being lashed by a squall, bands of rain pounding across the deck and the sea was in chaos. He motioned for them to turn around against the railing. There were three men and one woman. Behind him, the first mate had come out of the wheelhouse and was shouting. In a single, smooth motion the large man pivoted and shot him in the chest without hesitation. The first mate dropped to the deck without making a sound, the crewmen flinched at the shot and I felt my strength expand and thrum more deeply.

Some of the crewmen were whimpering and quietly pleading. With a professionalism I admired and no trace of reserve, the large man walked quickly down the line of crewman, punching a bullet into the back of each skull. The last couple didn't even try to run. He walked back pushing those bodies over the railing that hadn't already fallen into the churning sea. I was intoxicated, feeling god-like as the lightning split the sky around me.

I retrieved my focus and found the large man back inside the work room. He put a cigarette in his mouth and lit it with a brass lighter that he rubbed pensively as he smoked. There were self-destructive thoughts sublimating in his head that did not serve my purpose, so I easily led him back on deck to throw the gun overboard. Without this distraction, the large man lifted a red fuel can from the locker at the stern and went back inside, descending through a midship hatch. I confess I was drunk with the roiling, fierce energy that surged through me and too distracted by the possibilities of what lay ahead to pay close attention. After he had been gone some time, the large man rushed back on deck and unhitched the dinghy. He jumped into the small boat, pulled the engine to life and started to speed through the wild chop of the sea.

I could discern that he was trying to get to shore and that was something I encouraged. As I started to follow him I realized with horror that my physical body remained in the tank. I clawed my way into the large man's consciousness, compelling him to return to the vessel. He hesitated and I got a glimpse of something he had done, something he had trained to do in the past. Before I could force him to turn around, there was a loud blast from the large boat and a screech of metal. I sensed heat and flames, fearing my greed would be my ruin a second time.

Thankfully, I also sensed an inrushing of cold seawater, surging into the belly of the boat. The vessel listed and started to drop its bow into the towering waves. The rain poured through the man's grey-streaked hair and beard as he watched the boat succumb to the sea and allowed himself a single nod. I shared his relief as I felt the seawater engulf my body, which I hoped I would be free of for some time.

I firmly attached myself to this remarkable being and allowed his unique animal to diffuse into my spirit. I placed my mark upon him so I might find him again in time.

Once we made landfall, he found an anonymous bar and drank himself into a fury, leading to a blur of violence. Fueled by the sea killings, I left him to wander amongst the mortals, thrilling at their deviancy and engineering my cruelties. The power I had gained sustained me for a long time and I got quite lost in my exploits. However, my thoughts kept returning to the man, I sense we shared a similar history and he intrigued me. I searched for his frequencies but the faint tugging at my back had already begun. I cursed and yielded to the inevitable wrench.

I was mightily confused when I next became aware, back in my ugly shell. I was still in the tank on the boat but it was on an incline and contained debris, sand and a few small creatures besides myself. I sensed I was close to land but far from the tell-tale flitter of mortal frequencies. In time, I concluded that the sinking boat must have stayed afloat long enough for the storm to ground it upon some rocky shore. For now I was trapped and I had no choice but to wait, a pastime I was most familiar with.

The vibration of waves hitting the hull stirred great hope in my spirit. Eventually the waves found their way inside the wreck and replenished the stale water in the tank then continued to rise until wreck was full. With a great effort, I furiously paddled my feeble swimming legs to lift myself above the tank. I only managed a short rise before the confined space and debris barred my way. I tried many times but the result was always the same and I cursed with exhaustion. The tilted surface of the tank reappeared as the tide receded and there I stayed, with a few small creatures for company or food.

My frustration smoldered as every tide taunted me with freedom. On the rare occasion that I would sense a mortal nearby, they would idly regard the wreck but never came within striking distance, no matter how hard I willed it. I was trapped and impotent, like a djinn in a bottle.

Then came the boy. His frequencies broke through my torpor with a song I had heard before, yet his sung a variation that was lighter but more keen than that of the marked man. With a fearlessness I admired, he climbed onto the deck and did not hesitate to step down into the dark body of the wreck. I thrilled at connecting with the vital animal within as the boy moved closer and I easily slipped into his open, young mind. I drew him closer and encouraged him to lift the tangle of metal that covered the tank. He gasped when he saw me.

I weighed having him to carry me back to the sea but as soon as I looked into his eyes I realized what a rich vein of dark energy lay within my reach. I would wait a little longer.

14

They had walked for a long time and Coby was grumbling about being thirsty. For some reason Coby had decided to bring the quadruped and was shifting it from hand to hand, scowling at the pavement. They were in the burbs, way out in the West of the city, and they were lost in a glum development of affordable homes from the fifties. Every row and street looked the same. Jay checked the address on the crumpled napkin one more time and was relieved to spot a matching road sign. He tugged Coby's sleeve and they crossed the intersection to enter the street.

After counting off the even house numbers they arrived outside a modest townhouse. Jay had wondered if there would be a neon sign or a crystal ball in the window but this was an utterly unremarkable dwelling. The small front yard was featureless except for the immaculately trimmed lawn and the older, tan coupe that sat in the driveway, its paintwork gleaming. Jay double-checked the address but it was correct.

They walked up to the frosted glass door and pushed the doorbell. A beige-colored figure emerged from the gloom behind the glass and opened the door. William Crump was barely five feet tall, his auburn hair was precisely parted on the left of his prominent, pale forehead and his deep-set eyes were a curious shade of grey. He wore a beige sweater-vest over a shirt that had possibly been white at one time but had settled for something less colorful, and the type of slacks men of a certain age seemed to prefer. A pair of burgundy socks provided the only color in his ensemble. The man smiled, seemingly amused.

"Not what you were expecting? I get that a lot."

Jay was flustered by having being caught assessing the man.

"No, I mean, it's nice to meet you, William."

"Pleased to meet you too, I won't shake if you don't mind. Do come in, you can leave your shoes here by the door."

William motioned to a shoe rack and waited for them to pull off their sneakers and follow him down a hallway. They passed a room that was dark and empty except for a small angle-poise lamp illuminating a desk that held only a legal pad and several sharpened pencils. William led them into a living room that was no less austere. A brown, velour three-piece suite was arranged around a very old television in a polished wood cabinet, on the wall above, a kidney-shaped, walnut plaque held a clock, thermometer and barometer. Everything was spotless but there was a stale, metallic odor to the place. Jay figured that if William didn't like cologne, he probably didn't like air-freshener.

William turned to them, waving a hand towards the couch.

"Please, have a seat."

William perched on the edge of a lounge chair, while Jay and Coby shuffled to get comfortable on the spongy sofa cushions. Jay noticed that the only decoration in the room was a collection of small dachshund figurines on the side table.

"I like your Weiner dogs."

William smiled as he looked at them.

"Thank you."

"Do you have a dachshund?"

William chuckled.

"Oh, no."

William continued to look at the ceramic dogs with a pensive half-smile, then drew himself up and snapped his focus back to Jay.

"In the event that my information leads to a successful resolution, my fee is one hundred and eighty-three dollars and eighty-three cents. Is that acceptable?"

Jay frowned at the odd number but nodded his approval.

"Sure, that's fine."

"Good. May I please have the photograph of the target?"

Jay took the photo from his shirt pocket and handed it to William.

"This was when…"

William immediately held up a hand to silence him.

"Please, you must not tell me any details about the target, it can influence the work."

Jay held up his hands apologetically.

"Sorry."

"You were not to know."

William gestured to an archway that led to a small kitchen.

"There is water and soda in the fridge, feel free to have one, and please get comfortable as I might be some time."

With a quick, efficient smile, William turned on his heel and padded out of the living room in the direction of the spartan study. As soon as he was out of sight, Coby dashed into the kitchen and opened the old fridge. There was the telltale crack and hiss of a can being opened and Coby returned to flop on the sofa.

Jay watched him put his grubby socks on the coffee table then noticed it was a beer in his hand, not a soda.

"What the fuck are you doing?"

"He said to help ourselves."

"Not to beer for a minor!"

"Chill for fucksake, it's just one crappy beer."

Jay let his anger wash away. Coby had been through a lot and it wasn't like he hadn't snuck beers at thirteen himself. He changed the subject, lowering his voice.

"Hey, you think this weird dude is going to find anything?"

"Yeah, I bet he does. I saw a tv show about it, the government used guys like that to find Russian bases and stuff. It's pretty awesome."

"Really? Wow."

Jay thought that maybe he had heard something like that. Coby was becoming more animated, Jay suspected he had caught a buzz from the beer. He turned to face Jay with a serious expression.

"So, when we find Angela, we should go back home. Together."

A chill ran through Jay, this was a conversation he did not want to have.

"I hope we do find Angela but we can't go home."

"Why?"

Jay parsed through excuses and white lies but realized there was no point. He let out a long, slow sigh and looked over at Coby.

"You remember when dad used to be in the navy and did that weird special ops stuff he couldn't talk about?"

"Yeah?"

"Well, I think he had PTSD from whatever happened."

"You mean that thing where guys go crazy 'cos they saw too much bad shit?"

"Something like that. That's why dad would get weird and mean sometimes."

"Sometimes?"

Jay allowed himself a smile, the rest was going to be harder.

"Well, after you left, he got a lot worse. Mom was really anxious and he started to lean into the rum a bit harder. He started to freak out about going back to the rig for his next tour, something about the diving fed into his PTSD but he wouldn't talk to a shrink."

Coby was sitting upright with his fists balled into the sleeves of his red jacket, his beer forgotten and his eyes focused on Jay.

"Something happened on the rig and he got choppered home early. I think there was some sort of hearing and he got fired."

"But he hated that job anyway, right?"

"Yeah, he did, but all that stuff messed him up even more."

Coby pulled his knees up on the couch and stared at the curved black glass of the television. Jay watched his reflection for a moment, then continued.

"You remember he had that nine-millimeter he kept in the basement we weren't supposed to know about?"

Coby nodded.

"He used it to kill mom and to kill himself, but it didn't work."

"Why didn't it work?"

Coby's question was hardly audible in the silent room. Jay realized he was trembling and fought to control his voice.

"He kissed mom and put the gun to the back of her head. He tried to kill both of them with one bullet but it only got as far as his eye."

"What are you saying?"

"Mom died but dad lived, he was arrested and sent to prison."

Coby turned pale and his eyes bobbed around the room as if searching for meaning in what Jay had just said. He looked down at the quadruped still cradled in his lap and rubbed it with his thumb as he continued.

"How do you know all this?"

"Officer Willet. Dad called her after it happened to turn himself in. It took her a while to track me down but she did it. He was sentenced to life for first-degree murder and the house was put in my name. Later, she put me in touch with an attorney to sort out the paperwork and sell the house."

Coby shot him a dark look.

"You fucking sold it?"

"Sure, I wasn't going to go back there after what happened. I have plenty left, maybe we can use it to get a bigger place, so you can have your own room?"

Coby ignored this suggestion.

"So, there isn't a home left to go back to?"

"Sorry, it's all gone."

Coby's chin started to tremble, then fat tears whelmed from his eyes and he made no effort to dry them as they ran onto his shirt. A small painful moan escaped from his throat that turned into a snarl.

"I hate him, I fucking hate him!"

Jay gently pulled Coby into his chest and they sat that way for a long time until Coby's racking sobs eventually ebbed to silence.

The sun had dropped low in the sky by the time they heard the office door open and the swift approach of William's stockinged feet. The man's hair was matted to his forehead with perspiration and he looked physically exhausted as he walked into the room. Jay stood up, feeling doubtful about the single sheet of yellow note paper in William's hand.

"So, how did it go?"

William held his gaze with his unreadable grey eyes, then quietly sighed.

"It was a murky reading. The information comes in fragments, some of it may have meaning, some of it may not, some may be connected, some may not."

"Okay, I understand. What did you see?"

William looked down at the note paper and cleared his throat.

"I saw some vague things like sand and seaweed, maybe at night? An old lobster pot. I kept seeing a ship-in-a-bottle, perhaps more than one kind. The clearest image I got was a green metal buoy, it had a flashing light on top and the number 17 painted in white on the side."

William cocked his head expectantly but Jay's mind was a blank, he glanced at Coby but he was staring out of the window, lost in grief. Jay turned back to William.

"That's it?"

"I'm afraid so. I'm assuming none of that means anything to you at this time?"

"No, but I appreciate you trying. I'll send your fee if it does lead to something."

"I'd appreciate that, I'm sorry it wasn't clearer for you."

"No, really, it was good to have your help"

They put their shoes on in silence then Jay and William exchanged nods before they left. The fresh afternoon air felt good after the stuffy, stale atmosphere of William's house.

Coby hadn't spoken for a long time but suddenly gasped.

"I know where that place is."

Jay looked at him, trying to hide his skepticism.

"What do you mean?"

"The place William was describing with the green buoy, I know where it is. Come on, it's not far."

Jay watched Coby take off at a fast walk, the quadruped tucked under his arm and the oversize jacket billowing behind him. He seemed happier, so Jay jogged to catch up and decided to indulge him for a while.

15

I bewitched the boy with thrilling tales and flattery, while I probed his connection to the marked man. Such sweet poetry that I would be trapped by a man and his very son would free me. I marked him too for there are no coincidences, only the playful hand of fate.

I could feel the man's rage budding in the boy's adolescent body, whirling with his doubts and longings. I sensed the girl he desired was a touch-paper for him so I played my hand with caution. It was not long before he agreed to bring her.

Despite my grip on his tender, young mind he was not ready for what I had designed. No sweet seamstress moment for him. Yet I tried and the results were the same after the rage had been stoked. I watched the very last glimmer of life fade from her remarkable eyes as the seawater rose into the weak, shallow draft of her lungs. I soared away from the wretched vessel, expanding with the stolen energy. I was aware of my body tumbling on a current, pulled out of the boat and allowed to drift into a rocky crevasse to begin healing. I was also aware of the girl's body pulled along on the same strong current, a wisp of blood tracing from within the curls at the back of her head, her bright clothing fading into the green darkness.

After I had attached and followed him home, the boy betrayed his weakness further by clinging to his feeble mother like a starving kitten. She would need to be absent if he were to reach his potential. Nevertheless, the woman interested me, so very lost and downtrodden, endlessly mourning a marriage that had died on the vine and a life that had fallen to hopelessness.

I luxuriously drifted among the psyches around me, stirring up old anguish and creating new nightmares. The mother of the dead girl was terrified as she faced a life without her daughter, her lost husband already a tightly knitted scar. She would not allow her turbulent thoughts to settle for more than a moment, imploring her dead husband to help her. While all this distracted me, I was keenly aware of the marked man drawing closer. A subtle shift in his frequencies hinted a darker burden in his spirit since we had last engaged. As he approached, the boy's mother grew more anxious, memories of hurtful spat words and unexpected violence seeped into her tightly cupped mind. The boy was consumed with thoughts of the girl, he tortured himself because he had not returned to her.

I started to feel a weakening of my hold on the land but I knew the marked man was approaching. The woman was alone when he entered the house. She rushed to him, forcing a smile and awkwardly embracing him as he stiffened against her. She noticed the rum on his breath. He gave clipped answers to her questions until she sensed it was angering him and fell silent.

He pushed past her and found himself a drink in the kitchen. She tried to talk about the boy but he mumbled an interruption and took his glass of rum down the creaky stairs from the kitchen to the small basement below. I entered into his familiar spirit and marveled at the chaos.

The work that kept him alone in a suit at the bottom of the sea filled him with constant fear. Fear of something going wrong, fear of something in the darkness behind him. To keep himself going, he thought of the woman and boy, then his heart would collapse with the knowledge that he could never give them what they really sought. This was his world. Thirty terror-filled days on a cramped, metal island with no rum and bad memories, then a long ride home to face the people he did not know how to love. His only human connection were the men he fought until he lay spent on the metal floor, clumps of their hair between his fingers, his own blood in his beard. This was tragedy that only the human animal could create.

I willed him to open the case beneath the work bench and lift out the ugly, black pistol. It had none of the elegance of a fine katana but I presented it to him as a weapon of terrible beauty. I compelled him to see the simple, clean punctuation that such a device could exact on his life.

We were interrupted by a chime and a shuffle of noise at the main door. The man tucked the pistol into the back of his waistband and listened carefully. The voice of the female visitor instantly raised his ire and he reluctantly trod up the stairway.

There was a swirl of emotion between the two women that was too dense to decipher. The uniformed visitor noticed the glass of rum and the bulge under the back of the man's shirt as he silently looked out of the window. The boy returned and I took the opportunity to fan the flames of his guilt and paranoia, to chase him away, to rid myself of the visitor and her complications so I could focus on the man before it was too late. I could feel the familiar pull on my back build in strength and I grew enraged with frustration. Relief arrived when the boy succumbed to my will and fled. The visitor followed, imploring the mother to stay at home, that she would soon return with the boy.

With my time rapidly waning, I poured my will into the marked man. I forced him to turn and smile, to open his arms, to gently accept the woman who was trembling with fear into his arms. To look into her surprised eyes and tell her it would be okay, to lean down and kiss her on the mouth. A kiss that became deeper until she became completely still with submission. He reached behind his back and carefully raised the gun to the back of her head as they kissed. The woman's final thought was how good it felt to be intimate after all that time.

16

Jay was exhausted and thought longingly about the lounge, how wonderful it would be to drift away from all of this in a cool, dark room. He was surprised by how strong that desire was and how much it irritated him that it was out of his reach. He wondered what Valy was doing, he wondered if Valy knew he'd nearly killed him.

Coby had been silent for the last couple of miles, still striding along with purpose. They were walking through a run-down industrial area that backed onto the docks and the city shore, a short section of bleak, grey beach that drew few visitors. Coby cut across an intersection to a wide street lined with warehouses. The sea was visible at the far end in the last light of the falling sun, they walked towards it.

When Coby got to the end of the street, he turned to his right. Jay noticed that somewhere a pale green light was flashing and illuminating Coby's face with a green glow when it pulsed. Coby turned to Jay and smiled, waving him over.

There was a row of dark shop fronts, some were derelict and set between shuttered engineering places. In the center was a small, narrow store casting a golden glow on the sidewalk. A large metal buoy was hung in place of a sign, it was painted green with a white number seventeen on the front. The green light on the top steadily flashed on and off. As they drew closer, Jay saw that the window display was dominated by a large, black-lit aquarium, lined with sand and fronds of seaweed and filled with tiny iridescent fish. To one side, an old lobster pot was draped with seagrass jewelry and stacks of hand-made, glazed tiles and bowls were arranged across the front of the display. It was all beautifully made.

Suddenly, a mop of red curly hair appeared behind the aquarium as someone seemed to be climbing up to reach it. The girl was holding a can of fish food and was reaching down to open the aquarium lid when she spotted Coby. Her eyes widened and her mouth sprung open, her large teeth glowing eerily white in the spill from the black light.

"Angela! Angela!"

Coby was laughing and jumping up in front of the window. The girl left her fish food on the aquarium and jumped down, bursting out of the shop door a second later. Coby ran to meet her and hugged her fiercely, joyful tears in his eyes, she hugged him back, laughing.

"You're okay, you're really okay?"

"Yes, I'm fine, silly."

"But where did you go?"

"Oh, I just wandered off and got totally lost but this nice lady took care of me."

"I'm really sorry about our fight and breaking your pony."

"I'm sorry too and, it's okay, mom's making me another one."

Coby sighed happily and looked over at Jay.

"Can we hang out a bit?"

"Sure, of course."

"You're going to have to send William his money."

Jay nodded and smiled at the thought of the peculiar little man and his strange fee. He watched them cross the seafront street and sit on the seawall. Coby was showing Angela the quadruped and she ran a finger down its back, laughing at something Coby had said.

To give them some privacy, Jay wandered into the store, the door gave a little tinkle as he pushed it open. The store was just as tasteful as the window display suggested. Handmade textiles and pottery were arranged artfully on driftwood displays, the air smelled of sandalwood and the fresh-baked goods for sale on the counter. On one wall there was a large display of ships in a bottle, each one different and all of them incredibly detailed. One in particular caught his eye and he carefully picked it up to look closer. It was the wreck of a metal boat, listing over on some rocks. Its sides were streaked with rust and laced with seaweed. A tiny set of steps led belowdecks and when Jay angled the bottle he could just see into the hold, where two tiny figures, a boy and a girl, were looking at a white object on the sand between them.

"You picked my favorite one."

Jay turned to see who had spoken and his reply died in his throat. The woman was about his age and flawlessly beautiful. Her thick red hair was piled into a messy bun and her profoundly deep green eyes glittered from behind her cats-eye glasses. Her freckled cheeks were creased in a natural, dazzling smile. Before Jay could form a word in his dry throat, the woman's smile shifted to a circle of shock.

"Oh, my, god! What are you doing here?"

"Ah, college, I'm at city college. What about you?"

"I got sick of traveling and felt inspired, so I opened this place."

"It's wonderful, your pieces are so good."

"Thank you. It's really good to see you!"

Jay had so much to say, he didn't know where to start. His heart was beating hard in his chest and he felt himself flushing, so he hid his embarrassment by carefully sliding the ship back onto the shelf. When he looked back at the woman, her smile was gone and her expression was completely neutral, she seemed to be looking at something outside. Her vacant look shot a chill through Jay. He became aware of raised voices and turned to see that Coby and Angela were arguing over the quadruped, pulling it between them. Angela lost her grip and slammed into the seawall, the quadruped dropped to the pavement, shattering with a hiss of scattered fragments. Coby clenched his fists and shook with rage.

Jay ran to the door, jerked it open and lunged across the street towards Coby, just as the boy bent to pick up a metal bar from the pavement. He held it above his head over Angela, drops of water falling from the wet seaweed that clung to it. Jay tackled him, wrenching him to the ground by the loose fabric of the work shirt, just as Coby swung for Angela with the bar. Jay looked up, praying the bar hadn't hit the girl, but she was no longer by the wall. His head swiveled madly, trying to see where she had gone. Had she jumped over the wall?

Coby's strength was shocking as he writhed beneath him, flailing the bar behind him trying to hit Jay. Jay turned and shouted for the woman.

"Angela! Angela!"

The woman was no longer there, the store had become an empty, black maw in a derelict storefront. He felt Coby fall still beneath him and when he looked down saw the bar was gone and, instead of holding Coby, his fists contained two wads of fabric from the empty plaid shirt.

A cold wind plunged over the seawall as he struggled to make sense of the silence around him. He slowly stood and slipped on the shirt as protection from the chill wind. When he turned back towards the store, where the woman had previously stood, now stood the figure in the red suit.

Jay could feel the black thrum of anger vibrate in his chest, he was done with this. He walked across the street, his shoes crunching on the shards of the quadruped, and walked into the burnt-out store front.

He squared up to the figure, taking in the details of the childish, crude suit with the clown-like buttons. The bizarre shoes that looked like split hooves. The impassive, white mask regarding him silently.

"Who are you? What the fuck do you want?"

The figure swayed slightly but remained silent. Instead, it lifted it's mitten-covered hands and slowly raised the mask. Jay recoiled in horror when he found himself looking at the face of his father, his hair and beard dripping wet. Where his left eye had once been there was now a large, black void oozing sky-blue blood in a wet streak down his face.

Without saying a word, the man lifted his left hand and extended his thumb and first finger to make a gun. He then pushed the wool covered finger deep into the empty eye socket and pretended to shoot, miming the recoil. Jay watched with revulsion as a terrible grin spread across the man's face, showing a parade of broken yellow teeth within his greasy beard. A deep, wet, asthmatic laugh started to pump from the man's throat. An ugly sound that Jay barely remembered from childhood but one that was only ever used in the same mocking, sadistic way.

Jay lunged for the man, desperate to hurt him, desperate to make him pay for everything he had taken away. The man skillfully twisted out of his reach and sprinted down the corridor behind him, running deep into the dark bowels of the gutted building. Jay pounded after him, fueled by simmering rage. The man swung left at the end of the corridor, sliding his hand along the wall for balance and leaving a streak of blue blood on the plaster.

Jay took the corner to follow him but was stopped in his tracks by the sight of a small group of people in a windowless, dead-end room. There was a dimly-flickering brazier in the center, enough to see that his father was nowhere to be seen. Several bodies were slumbering on dirty mattresses, the others stood by the fire. A wiry young man with hollow cheeks approached him, his hands held out in front of him.

"Woah, man, you looking for someone?"

Jay blinked at him, struggling to keep up with this new shift. The man took a step back.

"You a cop?"

"No, I'm not a cop."

"Just in a hurry to get something, right?"

A gaunt woman in a sequined baseball cap snickered. Jay recognized the sharp, vinegary smell that hung in the air. The skinny man raised his ring-pierced eyebrows and started rifling through the pockets of his stretched-out hoodie.

The nagging desire he had felt on the walk across town had grown to the fill the void left by his depleted adrenaline. Its hungry claws raked at his chest, that old excitement building in expectation. He spoke without realizing he had decided to.

"You have any black tar?"

The dealer eyed him suspiciously, Jay wondered if he hadn't used the right name but the man seemed to recognize the genuine desire in Jay's eyes.

"You got money?"

"Yeah."

The dealer took a small twist of tin foil from his pocket and waved it at Jay.

"In that case, why, yes, I do, from the purest poppies in China, ten a gram."

The gaunt woman snickered again, the dealer clearly enjoyed an audience. Jay handed the man a bill and took the twist. As he did so, he locked eyes with a well-dressed, middle-aged man, the man immediately looked away, down to the briefcase at his feet. Jay didn't want to think too much about the man who clearly should have been somewhere else.

He found a seat on a bottle crate by the back wall and someone handed him a wad of tin foil and a lighter. He copied those around him, taking care with the the quantity of tar he put on the foil after the last time. The hot, acidic smoke caught in his throat but the effect was swift and powerful. As his mind tumbled backwards into oblivion, he heard the wet, rasping laugh of his father.

17

The uniformed woman returned to the wounded, marked man with medics and a storm of swirling thoughts. A missing girl, a runaway boy, a murder and an attempted suicide, all on one tiny, cliff-top lane. How her sharp mind glittered as it tried connecting and reconnecting the parts. I lamented that she would never know how my masterful hand was behind this symphonic tragedy.

The caravan of the dead and the living set off towards the city as I felt the marked man submit to the medicine in his veins and the bad dreams that waited. I turned my attention to the shimmering towers and thrilled at the possibilities. It had been a long time since I had enjoyed the multi-faceted distractions of a city, vibrating like a cathedral of a million desperate voices. I had so long been hobbled by rude fishing villages and bleak harbor towns, now my replenished spirit would allow me to sustain myself for a long time and leave my ugly, broken body to heal beneath the filthy rocks and sand.

The caravan arrived at a hospital and was swarmed by more people in uniform. I left them to their tiresome wittering and drifted into the rich chaos of the city streets. I was titillated by the common hatred and casual violence. There were those that hated others for the color of their skin, the gods they worshipped, their wealth or their poverty, the politicians they supported and the causes they didn't. Some were hated for being with men, or women, or both, or neither. Lives were impassively dispatched for a trifle or a sleight. These were nourishing grounds for the likes of me.

The boy came, as I knew he would. It was the marked man's turn to to be trapped in a small, ugly box, in which I took more than a little pleasure.

I roared around the bars and the money lenders, the strip clubs and the drug dens, gorging myself on pleasure, but I would always seek out that special, marked boy. I squatted on his back and whispered into his dreams about my dark plans, and stoked that flowering rage until he lashed out again and again.

As my unwitting acolyte matured he grew adept at concealing certain memories. Those moments when the leash of his anger slipped from his fingers and he allowed himself a moment of cruel violence before snapping it taut. He hid those memories beneath his obsessions and solitude and, eventually, intoxication.

He was an amusing diversion in this long journey but I grew weary. I was nearly free of that vile, squat body and I had a kingdom to rule. It was time to play my hand in this old game.

18

Jay was vaguely aware of someone pulling on the front of his jeans. He forced himself to swim up from the tar pits of sleep and found a man hunched over him, trying to unbutton Jay's fly. In the ember-light of the dying fire, Jay could see it was the businessman from last night, now looking disheveled and wild-eyed. Panicked, Jay lashed out with his right foot, landing a strong kick in the man's chest and sending him tumbling backwards. The man lay gasping between curse words as Jay found his feet. The dealer and most of the others had gone, just a few nodding forms remained on the mattresses. Jay steadied himself on the wall and found his way to the shop front.

There was a heavy fog shrouding the seafront and the flat, grey light gave no indication of the time of day. As he crossed the street to the seawall, his feet crunched over the tiny fragments that still remained of the quadruped. He slumped on the wall, feeling sick and wretched. His limbs were made of stone and his temples pounded. A sharp, sour odor drew his attention to the trail of vomit down the front of his t-shirt. He forced himself to stand and walk along the seafront towards his apartment.

The road was familiar to him because of the structure that started to materialize out of the roiling mist ahead. The city prison ship was an unapologetically brutal, grey structure that loomed over the dock behind several razor-wire perimeter fences. Jay stopped at his usual vantage point, an apex on the seawall before the road dropped steeply to the ship's dock. He scanned each of the tiny windows, looking for a sign. As he did so, the fractured thoughts and emotions that jittered in his mind condensed to a single, simple plan. It was all he had but it was all he needed, and it carried him the three miles home.

After a hurried shower, Jay rustled through a drawer to find a creased document then pulled up the prison contact page on his laptop. He dialed the number and a bored-sounding woman answered.

"Robert Sheffield Correctional Center, how may I assist you?"

"I want to check if an inmate is available for visitation."

"I need his name and prisoner number."

Jay read the information from the document.

"Yeah, that prisoner is… Oh, wait. Please hold for a second."

Jay's scalp prickled and he looked nervously at the dark space behind the bathroom door. The phone line clicked back open.

"Sorry, yes, he is at this facility but he was moved to the infirmary."

"Would I be able to visit him?"

"Are you family?"

"I'm his son."

"Did you fill in the visitor application that was sent?"

"Yes."

"There are visiting hours this evening at six-thirty but you should have applied two days ago. Plus he's in the infirmary. Let me talk to the warden's office, hang on."

Strangely inappropriate synth music swelled on the empty line. Jay watched the rain streak down his window, not allowing himself to think, only to move forward. After a while, the line crackled back to life.

"Okay, lucky for you the warden has made an exception and I can schedule you for this evening. Have you visited before?"

"No."

"Be at the visitor check-in at six, bring ID, no weapons, no drugs, no contraband. Can I help you with anything else?"

"No. Thank you."

"Have a blessed day."

Jay checked the window of the studio doors before he entered. The room seemed empty but a figure appeared out of the dark storage room, making him start.

"What's up, Jay?"

Dylan's beard was now plaited and his scarves had been switched for a shawl. The laundry basket he was carrying was filled with ceramic heads.

"Hey, Elon, is Lutkin around?"

"I'm Dylan, man. Lutkin's at a conference until next week. You okay? You look kinda…"

Jay ignored him, turning his attention to the shelf in his locker. Dylan shrugged and backed through the doors with his basket. Jay found what he was looking for. The plain porcelain tile was about six inches long, an inch wide, and maybe a quarter-inch thick. It was a leftover from some firing tests earlier in the year.

Jay walked down to the far end of the studio and the deserted glassblowing area. He spun up the lap grinder, ran the water and began grinding the long edges of the tile. Working by intuition, the task consumed him as moved up grits on the wheel's surface, creating a sharper and sharper edge. Noticing the time on the studio clock, he made a few more passes on the wheel and wiped the blade clean on his sleeve. He tested its edge by laying his open jacket on the bench and felt it cut effortlessly through the lining under the collar. He fixed it in place between the layers of fabric with duct tape. When he pulled on the jacket the knife sat concealed between his shoulder blades.

Jay did not allow himself to think during the metro ride out to the docks. He only allowed himself to move forward, watching the landscape shift further and further downmarket until the last stop on the line.

Jay made his way to the visitor building, signed in and got ushered through screening. He walked through both metal detectors and retrieved his wallet and keys from the plastic bowl. There were few people occupying the plastic seats in the concrete-block waiting area.

As he sat under the buzzing, harsh lights, Jay's emotions began to waver. A deep anger would begin to rise only to be met by a wave of queasy panic. He closed his eyes and sought the horizon, the clear way forward.

"Sir?"

Jay's eyes shot open and focused on the young, prison guard standing over him, smiling patiently.

"Yes?"

"I'm Officer Hernandez, I'm going to escort you up to the infirmary."

"Yes, thank you."

Jay followed the man through several gates that buzzed with electric locks as they passed. An inclined corridor indicated they were boarding the ship itself, then more gates led to endless corridors.

"It's all the way in back I'm afraid, sir."

"That's okay. I appreciate it."

As gate after gate closed, Jay's panic started to rise again, propelled by the angry shouts of men reverberating through the ship's duct system. Finally, they reached a red cross symbol painted on the bulkhead and buzzed through the door. There was a short corridor with a half-dozen doorways. The guard indicated to the one nearest.

"You can go on in, he's expecting you. I'm going to be here in this seat if you need anything."

The man had soft, compassionate eyes and a sincere smile. Jay got the impression he embraced his job as a calling and was grateful that he would be the person to whom he would surrender.

Jay's heart thundered in his chest as he opened the door. Unlike his hospital room, this was much smaller, with old, chipped fittings and no windows at all. He forced himself to meet the gaze of the figure in the bed.

His father's hair and beard were completely grey and he seemed so much smaller than Jay remembered. The weight loss was clear in his sunken cheeks and thin wrists, hanging in shackles locked to the hospital bed frame.

There was a cannula in his nose and an IV tube in his arm. His left eye was covered in a black eye-patch, the other was dark-rimmed and jaundiced but fiercely staring back at him.

"Shit, boy, you look worse than me."

The laugh was still recognizable but fragile and insubstantial, like dry leaves.

"What's wrong with you?"

"Cancer, I'm full of it, eating me alive. Doc says it won't be long."

Jay felt his horizon tilt but he grasped at the tendrils of anger that clawed in his throat, acknowledged the weight of the blade that lay down the back of his neck.

"You deserve it, you killed mom. You were going to leave me an orphan."

His father's eye gradually lost its defiant glint and looked down at his withered hands.

"I do. I do deserve it. I have done terrible things in my life and that was the worst of them."

Jay felt like he was seeing his father for the first time. A tiny, broken, tortured man who was about to leave this world alone in a windowless metal box.

"Why did you do it?"

"Because I couldn't stand to be with her and I couldn't stand to be without her. And I fucked it up. I'm sorry."

Jay held his father's gaze for a long moment.

"Did you love her?"

His father's eye welled with tears and looked away.

"Oh, god, I loved her so much."

He hid his cracking voice in a cough and wiped the tears on his shoulder. He cleared his throat and met Jay's gaze again.

"I signed the house over to you, you saw that?"

"Yes, I sold it."

"Hey, it was your house, I was never going to be able to live there again anyway. They ever find that girl?"

"No. Officer Willet told me it was ruled as an accidental death."

His father bent forward to reach his shackled hands and scratch his beard. The chain chattered against the rail.

"She thought I did it."

"Who?"

"Willet thought I'd killed the little girl, raped her."

"Why?"

"I have a rap sheet, tried to off myself… I didn't, by the way."

Jay watched his dad wince at some hidden agony, his jaw working to quell it, his elbows nursing his sides. It passed and Jay caught his eye.

"I know you didn't."

"Good."

"I'm going to go now, Dad."

His father nodded, seeming somehow smaller and almost child-like.

"Okay, bye, Coby."

"Bye, Dad."

The kind, young guard seemed surprised that the visit had been so short but politely escorted Jay back through the labyrinth of gates and corridors to the visitor exit. He hesitated a moment as he held the door open, then decided to speak.

"It's wonderful that you came to visit your father tonight. You were the only person on his visitor list and every day after you sent back the visitation paperwork, he would ask if you were coming that visit day, every time. Since he got sick it was really important for him to say goodbye to you, so, thank you, from someone who didn't get to do the same."

The young man held out his hand and Jay shook it, lost for words.

Jay pumped his aching legs up the steep road from the dock to the crest of the seawall. As he approached the summit, he noticed a path of wet, comma-shaped footprints leading to his old vantage point. At their conclusion was the red-suited figure, slouched on the seawall.

A long-forgotten, scratchy rumble worked its way into his head, followed by shifting images and, finally, words.

"Hi, Coby, how you holding up?"

Jay straightened and walked slowly towards the creature, which stood in response and jabbed a mittened finger towards him.

"You should have killed him. It was too easy, chained to the bed with the guard outside. You fucking pussy."

Jay stood directly in front of the figure and noticed how it swaggered back and forth, trying to seem aggressive.

"What happened to the samurai demon speeches, Kabu?"

"Oh, Coby, you have such a wonderful imagination, dreaming up all those nasty killings, you little sicko."

"That's right and you were just a made-up doll in a comic book. You were useless, you never helped me, you didn't help me find Angela."

Kabu raised his mittened finger again.

"You know where Angela is, you have the photo. That boat trip with your mom? Remember that green buoy in the background, number seventeen? Those lovely, big teeth are not white any more, not at the bottom of the shipping channel in the filthy mud. That little cracked skull that never had a chance to heal. You left her down there on her own, just like you left your mom at the bottom of her grave without even being there to say goodbye."

Jay felt the familiar black vibration pulse and build in his chest. He let the emotion fall from his face and allowed the rage to surge through him. He grabbed Kabu by the throat and felt the muscles in his neck writhe and quiver as he squeezed. The spines that ran along the bottom of his mask undulated as if trying to reach Jay's hands. His mittened claws snatched at Jay's forearms and his split-hoofed feet slid and skittered on the pavement. Jay bore down harder on his grip, repulsed by the muscles on Kabu's chest and forearms convulsing like snakes.

As he felt Kabu's grip on his arms fade, Jay freed his right hand and reached behind his collar to pull the porcelain blade from its hiding place. With a single, swift motion he plunged it deep into Kabu's left eye.

Kabu froze, trembled violently for a few seconds, then tumbled backwards over the seawall. Jay lunged forward to watch him fall onto the rocks below. His white mask shattered with a hiss and his red suit dissolved onto the rocks as scores of eyeless black eels slithered out and escaped into the crevices below.

An oily, grey wave washed over the rocks and receded. A tattered, red fertilizer bag, caught on a split stone, undulated in the flowing water. A horseshoe crab shell lay nearby, jammed between two rocks and bleached white by years in the sun.

Jacob walked down to the modest stretch of beach. The evening sky had cleared and a waxing gibbous moon laid its silver path on the bay. Tomorrow he would take William Crump his fee and then visit Officer Willet. He surprised himself by spinning a couple of times as he crossed the moonlit beach.

Printed in Great Britain
by Amazon